GIVEN

PROJECT XOL
BOOK SIX

AMABEL DANIELS

COPYRIGHT AND DISCLAIMER

This is a work of fiction. Names, characters, businesses, places, events, and incidents are either the products of the author's imagination or used in a fictitious manner. Any resemblance to actual persons, living or dead, or actual events is purely coincidental.

ISBN: 9798649306058

DEDICATION

For Dr. Stacy Philpott, the woman who introduced me to the world of scientific research.

CHAPTER ONE

CASSIDY

Fight or flight.

I'd done both, dammit. And I was still screwed.

When the Xol monster had rushed at me, all demonic scowl and too many muscles, I'd resisted. I'd feigned surrender and let him tackle me sideways, and as I'd rolled away, I'd kicked as hard as I could at his jaw. That was all the physical violence I could think of that quickly.

Then I ran. Away was my only goal, but even with that reaction, I hadn't improved my odds. He'd caught me again and stuck me with that damn gun.

I didn't know how long I'd been out or where I was, but I fumed. Fight *and* flight, and I was *still* the prey. If my body's instincts hadn't helped save me, I didn't know what would. That I needed help of some kind was given. Because alone and handcuffed in the cargo space of some kind of moving vehicle, I was out of tricks. And rescuers.

Luke. I swallowed around a lump in my throat. *Luke.* He wasn't here with me. While I missed him, and needed to borrow his strength and let his anger and confidence rub off on me, I was thankful he wasn't cuffed at my side. I didn't want to bring the man I loved into this uncertain danger. Whatever I was heading to…

I squinted my eyes shut tight. Tears weren't going to do a single thing for me now. It wasn't easy to ward off the sting and heat behind my lids, though. Just knowing Tami had me and planned something bad spelled disaster. Taking shaky but steady breaths, I fought the rising need to throw up. My arms began to tremble a little as the anxiety blanketed me. Confrontations always wrecked me into a nervous mess, but I just couldn't afford it.

Be strong. Just...don't give in to it.

Instead of wishing for Luke's help, I focused on me. On here. A slight gas smell floated in the air, like I was near an engine. My back and butt were stiff from being slouched against the metal floor and wall for who knew how long. On my arm, I felt the residual sting of the needle where that Xol freak had tranqed me. He hadn't been gentle about it. The unrelenting drone of humming dominated my senses. I was being transported in something. More than anything, I could ride out the dips and bumps of motion.

I opened my eyes and sucked in another deep breath. The panic attack faded even more as I scanned my surroundings once more. Viewing the cargo space gave me a better sense of...doing. Freaking out wouldn't get me anywhere. Scoping out the place and maybe finding an escape or weapon would.

Metal floor and white-painted metal walls caged in to make a narrow room. I wasn't captive in too big of a space, and coupled with the motion I felt, I couldn't gauge if I was in a van, boat, or plane.

It has to be a plane. We dipped low again. No rut in a road or a smack against a wake. I was on a damn plane. I could be taken anywhere and no one would be able to find me. Fear spiked again but I swallowed hard and concentrated on where I was *now.*

I couldn't spot a door. Or much of anything. At least there was some light to show me my scant options of a plan.

The more I tried to resist a full-out panic, the more I considered the idea I was lucky to stall here like this, to remember what had happened and guess what might come next. Michael had taunted me, wanting the last beta subspecies vial in exchange for letting me see Rosa. They had her—Tami and those Project Xol scientists had taken my mother.

How long had they had her?

Were they hurting her? *More* torture?

Where did they find her?

I was eager to see Rosa after all of her enigmatic messages for help. Of course, I wanted to see her, just not like this.

Freaking Michael. He just had to come back and get me. When I'd faced off the huge man who'd tried to capture me from the beginning, I knew not to give in to his plans. Rosa wouldn't want me to surrender. Doing so would be the ultimate failure. She'd trusted me to retrieve Scott's data and seek out the vial—to prevent Tami from obtaining the resources she needed—and I'd be damned if I let her down.

Only…I *had* failed. I couldn't run fast enough, couldn't outpower a man who'd been pumped with regenerative DNA and amped up with a hormone frenzy.

Luke had been holding Michael back from getting the vial. Elena—

Why didn't she just smash it? I ground my teeth, my annoyance at that woman rising higher. As soon as she saw the Xol guys show up, why hadn't she opened that casing and broken that vial? It was what they'd been after all along.

Well, that vial and *me*, apparently.

I felt for her, despite her antagonist attitude, when the other Xol mutant had attacked her. I'd only witnessed it in a blur of action, fleeing myself, but I wasn't so coldhearted to wish her any pain. Maybe she couldn't free herself from the attack long enough to destroy the vial in her hand. I'd been at the mercy of Xol freaks attacking me to know they were *very* formidable fighters.

Do they have it now? I surveyed the space again, wondering if they'd succeeded and had taken the vial from her in the end. If I could find it and finally do the deed of breaking it, that'd be one point for Team No Regenerative Killer Freaks. And if they didn't have it on this plane, less than forty-eight hours were left before the vial would be useless.

Maybe Luke and Tramer can stall them? Until the vial is kaput? No. I shook my head. Stalling Xols would be too dangerous for mere mortals like my man and for Tramer as well.

Tramer. What had happened to him? He was so logical about all of this, surviving and beating whatever came his way. If only we'd heeded his advice, to prioritize destroying the vial. Shame seeped in, my cheeks burning a bit as I remembered how and why we'd stalled dealing with the last vial.

Perhaps it was juvenile of me to waste time and argue with Elena so stubbornly. Or not. Following my instincts, I'd stood my ground when Elena was difficult. She'd wanted to take charge and kill all the subspecies. I was all for stopping Tami, but until I knew more, and that such deaths were the *last* option, I wasn't going to bend to her will. I only wished I'd been firmer, and flat-out told her *no*. It all happened so fast, hearing what the vial and Scott's code stood for. It was too big to wrap my head around to make such lasting decisions. I'd needed more time to make sense of it, but regardless of the confusion, I knew I'd do whatever was necessary to stop Tami.

I snorted a laugh at myself, almost irritated at my weak, nagging hope. That if we destroyed the subspecies, there would be no chance at what Rosa,

Scott, and Hendrick had researched long ago. While I was more than aware of the dangers of Project Xol, the fledging optimist in me still hung on to a feeble what-if, clinging to an idea that a *real* cure for cancer might still be in our grasp.

I huffed again, shoving that farfetched dream aside.

At the noise, another came, almost in response to mine.

Tensing, alarmed at the idea I might not be alone back here after all, I jerked to face the direction from where the sound came.

A cough. Weak, but there.

Inhaling as calmly as I could, I craned to see past a stack of duffel bags lining the floor. Large black canvas shapes. Some were fat and stocky and others were long. The linear ones suggested they carried long guns, and I bet I was spying the Xols' ammo and gun stock.

At the end of the line of bags, something else stood up. Beyond the slight wall of bags was something sticking upright. Covered in white, it almost looked like…

I narrowed my eyes, straining my eyesight after the grogginess of the sedative and the beating of the panic attack.

Feet?

I blinked and nearly toppled to my side, trying to get closer to see. Only, I'd craned too far over and I fell. Instead of something holding me back like I expected of the cuffs at my wrists, there was slack.

Huh?

God. How much of an idiot could I be? Trapped in a cargo space on a plane and I hadn't even tested my cuffs yet? Sure, I couldn't just waltz out of here, but I loathed that I was so quick to mentally forfeit myself to the fact I was restrained in here.

Rolling to my knees and hands, I pushed up. A chain was locked to me all right. One end of the links ended at a hook on the wall. I could stand, thankful now at the realization my legs weren't shackled. I took a few steps from where I'd been sitting and followed the length of the chain. There was enough to allow me quite some distance. I bet this chain was usually used for strapping large objects to the ground.

Holding the bulk of chain—surprisingly lightweight in my hands—I slowly approached whatever lay beyond the line of bags. I panted, getting more worked up by the second as I came closer.

They were feet. I followed the lines of legs, thick, muscular calves and thighs outlined under the sheet. A beast of a man. I continued coming closer. A calmly rising and falling wide chest. Even his pecs were visible through the contours of the fabric. Broad shoulders…

I crept the last few inches toward him and couldn't hold in a gasp.

He opened his eyes and glowered at me. Nothing else. Lying there still as a statue, he seemed to be made of stone, only able to open his eyes. The furious intensity of hatred there chilled me.

"Are you kidding me?" I muttered it to myself as I stepped back.

There was *no* way… I swallowed hard and reared back again. No way? Hardly. Tami had defied the rules of reality by creating regenerative mutants. Normally, there would be absolutely no way a human body could be alive after falling out of an airplane.

"No." I didn't want to believe it. Even after witnessing Michael surviving head trauma, gunshots, knife wounds and still leaving, it was just that hard to accept.

Looking at Ryan on a makeshift gurney had to be a hallucination.

"Planning to shove me out the door again?" he jeered.

I flinched at his rough voice. I assumed he was paralyzed here, so still. I began to shake, too many ugly visuals blasting through my mind. How a body would be after impacting the earth. Blood, broken bones, the gore and destruction of a human body.

He crinkled his eyes in a sneer at my shuddering. "You better be scared. Because I *always* get my revenge."

I stepped back again. This…monster that couldn't be stopped. It was like diving into cold water, the fact of how scary Tami's science could be. The longer mutants like Ryan lived on earth, no one would be safe.

"You and that fucker. Luke?" He let out a grunt of a laugh. "Both of you. You won't get away with this."

I gritted my teeth. Him mentioning Luke's name was all it took to chase away some of my all-encompassing fear. Luke? No, Ryan wasn't going to finish things off with my man. Not if I had anything to do with it.

He coughed again then said, "Once she's done with you, I'll have *my* fun and make him watch."

Luke's not here. Luke is safe. Luke is— I swallowed hard, refusing to let Ryan see how much he was getting to me. Because even if Luke was still in Mexico, I didn't doubt Project Xol could find him again. Even worse, if I knew Luke as well as I did, there was every chance he was chasing after *me*.

"I'll make him watch as I kill you. Before I finally end him."

I couldn't speak. He seemed to take my silence as surrender because he continued goading me. "As soon as she's done using you—"

"What does she want with me?" I cut off his boisterous goals.

Truly a wicked soul, he let me keep on wondering and worrying as the plane began to descend. He chuckled a weak and ugly sound and said no more.

CHAPTER TWO

LUKE

I slammed the van's gear stick into park.

It wasn't enough. I punched the steering wheel. A crack sounded in the dash.

Heaving out a breath, I hung my head. Defeat. So this was what it felt like.

I lost her.

The van engine idled low and I feared the vehicle would stall.

If it did, then what would it matter? I'd lost Cassidy.

As soon as I saw that Xol mutant taking her onto the ATV, I gave chase. He'd been too elusive, weaving that ATV through the woodline, easily wedging between trees. Running would have gotten me nowhere, so I'd jumped in the van. This fat, clunky, outdated van that couldn't keep up with the slimmer vehicle designed for off-roading.

Once I'd heard the thumping of helicopter blades, I knew it was over. I'd driven as hard and fast as I could in the direction that asshole had taken her, but I was too slow, too late. A chopper rose above the tree canopy and that sealed it.

Project Xol had taken her.

I failed her. That gorgeous, gold-hearted, sassy spitfire who'd chosen me, who'd wanted *me*. I'd only just come to respect and accept that she had my heart, that I loved her. And now she was gone. Just like that, taken.

"Dammit!" I roared at the still forest surrounding me.

Birds flittered off their perches on trees and I closed my eyes tight. The depth of my agony threatened tunnel vision, replaying the image of her being carried away like a limp burden. I couldn't. I couldn't accept this. I—

No whining. No wallowing. I gritted my teeth and fisted a tight grip on the steering wheel. All right. It was useless to complain. I'd been in shitty conditions before and I was still standing. My life had never mattered, lacking meaning until I met Cassidy. But now that she was my reason to fight, I would.

Tramer's advice from the cartel's compound sounded again.

Don't think. Don't dwell. Just go.

I had to move. Even if they had a head start, flying through the air to God knew where, I wasn't giving up.

Move it.

I unclenched my hands and retightened a looser hold on the wheel. Move where, though? How?

Tramer. I was too used to going through life solo or looking out for others. It was hard to remember I had an ally in this. The Special Forces retiree had taken off through the woods, after the Xol who'd been holding that vial case.

It killed me to turn away from the direction where Cassidy had been taken, but unless I could sprout wings and fly, staring after the woods would make me nothing but a lovesick moron. If I loved Cassidy as much as I thought I did, then I'd help her. And backtracking to seek Tramer's aid was the only productive thing I could do.

I reversed and headed back toward the nature refuge Elena had brought us to. It looked just the same, even though so much violence had just occurred out back. I drove past the structure, heading the way Tramer had gone on foot.

On foot. I shook my head, admiring the tenacity that man had. He'd been stabbed in the damn foot but he'd been confident enough to pursue a regenerative mutant. It had to be confidence, and not stupidity, that drove Tramer to action. He was too wise to react irrationally.

I couldn't get far in the woods. There was hardly a path to begin with. After the vehicle slammed down following a rut—or maybe it was a fallen tree—a loud cranking noise accompanied me.

"I'm getting nowhere." Just like my pursuit after the Xol who'd taken Cassidy on the ATV, my mode of transportation was holding me back. This van wasn't cut for curving journeys through the woods. It didn't seem like it was cut for holding out much longer, period. If I killed this van, I'd be stuck to my own two feet. Preserving my resources out here was crucial.

Even if I was alone in finding Cassidy—

Alone at finding someone? When had I ever been alone since I met Cassidy? We'd had constant help at searching people.

Zero.

He'd been helping us from the beginning. Looking for Rosa, Hendrick, and intel on people in my and Cassidy's past. *He sure as hell better have a location for Tami by now*. I could call him. Cassidy's backpack had been lost in the scuffle behind Elena's refuge.

Elena. She had to be dead by now. I'd left Michael back there as well. I hated the vulnerability of turning my back on my enemy, but going after Cassidy had been first.

After what felt like fifty turns, I finally backed out of the tight spot I'd trapped the van in. I returned to the refuge. Gun at the ready, I ran back toward the water.

No one. Nothing. Not a soul was in sight.

I rubbed at my face, scoping the area for anyone who might be hiding.

I was alone. Elena had been lying just over there, gasping and bleeding from a knife to the chest. She'd implored me to get the vial. As if I'd ever put Cassidy as a lower priority,

The Xol that had attacked Tramer—he'd been down and seemingly dead. His body no longer lay on the grass.

Michael… I stared at the spot where he'd fallen. I'd tranqed him and he'd gone down immediately. I hadn't expected that reaction, but he must have been toting something uniquely potent that it could bring his regenerative ass down. He wasn't there.

Most importantly, Cassidy's backpack was absent too.

"Now what?" I returned to the van. Lingering out here wouldn't do anything.

As I shoved into the driver's seat, hope soared. My heart raced faster at the sight of a phone plugged into the charger. I wasn't out of luck just yet.

Rubbing at a sore spot on my ribs where Michael had beat me, I sighed and dialed. It was Tramer's phone. No matter. It was a burner that could lead me to Zero.

He picked up after three rings. The dial tone ended but nothing followed.

I frowned, wondering why he wasn't speaking.

"Zero?"

A whoosh of air came over the line.

"Thank *God*."

Alarm flooded my system.

"Someone called on Cassie's phone minutes ago," he said.

Michael! I held back a growl.

"I knew something was up. I terminated the call and ended that trail. Are we compromised? Is she?"

"She was taken."

"What!"

I closed my eyes, hearing the accusation in his voice. He blamed me.

"They came for us."

"Where?" Noises of something shuffling sounded next. "Where's Tramer?"

"He took off after the vial."

"Goddammit! Who has Cassidy?" he asked.

"Xol. Michael showed up and Elena was being...difficult, arguing with Cassidy and—"

Zero growled. "Fine. Fine. Hold on. I'll see if I can find her."

"Cassidy?" I huffed. "She's in a helicopter the last I saw."

"That's fine."

I gripped the phone so hard I feared I'd crack it. "That's not fine!" I didn't doubt his concern for his friend but hearing such blunt words tore at me. *I wouldn't be fine until she was at my side again.*

"I mean, it doesn't matter if she's in the air or on land. I can still get a location on her."

I gaped at nothing, trying to process his words. Zero had some insane skills behind the screen, but…

"T-man gave her a tracker. Both of you, actually."

I opened and closed my mouth, shocked at this news. Tramer put trackers on us? It felt…sneaky.

"We wanted to make sure nothing would happen if you were to split up."

When? How? I hadn't felt anything. "What—"

The incredulousness of my tone must have said more than enough. "Didn't he give you a small switchblade?" He hummed for a few seconds. "Yeah. He did. I got your location right here."

"That knife?" He'd slipped it into my shoe when we were captured by the cartel. I'd assumed he'd given it to me for the purpose of a blade.

"Okay. Head west," he said, likely consulting a map on his screen. The fact I had a tether to him helped. Knowing Cassidy's location was traceable made me feel even better. "May as well head toward the city. If they're in the air, you need to get there too."

I jimmied the gearstick into drive and sped from the refuge. "Where is Cassidy?"

"Heading northwest. They've already got her over the border."

Back to the States? At least I wouldn't have to contend with the cartel there.

"What about Tramer?"

"No clue. He didn't have another tracker for himself. The phone you're using was supposed to be my connection to him."

Foolish move. Then again, it wasn't like we'd had much time to prep for all the worst-case scenarios and stock up on trackers or anything of the kind.

"Now tell me what the hell happened," he ordered, "while I try to find him in real time. How long has he been running and which way?"

"He headed east. Maybe twenty minutes ago?" I said. Then I gave him an abbreviated summary of what happened.

"Where's Elena?" he asked.

"No clue. Maybe they dumped her in the water?"

Zero scoffed. "I'm going to keep looking for T-man. But we need to get you back here and on Cassidy's trail before she loses that tracker."

I nodded, instinctively ducking as I drove under a low tree branch, even though it couldn't hit me through the van's roof. "Okay."

"You didn't have a warrant, so it shouldn't be as much of a problem."

"Except the fact everything's gone." If Michael had Cassidy's backpack, he had everything. My wallet, the money Zero had wired us, the passports.

"I'll…figure something out." He exhaled hard. "Just keep driving toward the city. I gotta keep an eye on where Tramer might be headed. You're going to head to the airport, I can tell you that much."

"And flying where?" It was imperative to watch where Cassidy was headed, but a destination would give me something to plan for. If I were to lose touch with Zero, I needed to know how to finish this on my own.

CHAPTER THREE

CASSIDY

When the plane landed, I braced myself for more violence. Or another tranquilizer. Neither sounded good. I was sore and edgy, still feeling the effects of fighting at the refuge and the drug they'd given me. I was more alert and clear-minded, but neither of those were any kind of a defense to what may come next.

When the cargo door slid open, though, I was greeted by someone familiar.

I never wanted to see Jolene again, but there she was, immaculately styled in another power suit.

Smirking at me and waving at me in a cutesy style. The skin of her hand and forearm was flawlessly smooth, not what could be expected from when I'd last encountered her holding flames. She was clear of any burn scars.

"Long time, no see," she teased.

"Fuck off," I replied. I had no choice but to be here under their power, but it didn't mean I had to be nice about it.

Two Xol freaks came to her side, forming a barricade of mutant humans in a hallway of some sort. Oh, as if my dinky little mortal self was such a threat. I wasn't in control and the need for backup was laughable.

Jolene's stare turned frosty but her smile curved up. Like she knew something I didn't. In fact, I guaranteed she knew many things I was in the dark about. And I wasn't eager to face my fate here. "This way," she ordered, beckoning me to come toward her.

I deadpanned at her as I walked out of the cargo space. I didn't need the guns pointing at me for a cue to move. I'd obey for now. Once I'd gone as far as my chain could allow me, I jingled my cuffs at her and raised a brow.

"Oh. Right." She strode toward me, swaying her hips side to side. Her black high heels clicked on the metal floor as she approached me.

Keeping her steely glare on me, she smiled like I was a fool. She gripped the chain, wrapped it around her dainty, delicate-looking hands, and pulled. The links broke apart easily. Still with that haughty smirk locked on me, she opened her fingers and let the broken chain fall with a clang to the ground.

Okay. Display of power. Noted, bitch. I swallowed. Hard. I didn't need her showing off to remind me that I was the weaker one here. I bet she'd wished that was my neck for how I'd gotten away from her before.

"This way," she repeated with too smug of a tone, walking away from me and into whatever building we'd arrived at.

The two Xol men parted to let her sashay down the hall. With my hands still cuffed together but no longer chained to the plane, I disembarked and followed her.

The corridor was devoid of color and style. No decorations. Beige paint. Linoleum on the floor. A sterile walkway that sloped down from the point where I'd exited the cargo space. I wasn't stupid enough to think we were at any airport.

She walked briskly, and with my hands bound together and in front of me, my gait was off. No. Something else… I schooled my face to remain blank as I concentrated on the slight pain in my foot. Pain? More like something was stuck—

In my shoe! Tramer had given me that slim knife and I'd forgotten about it in there. No one had frisked me for weapons or anything else. Even if they had when I'd been out, they wouldn't have left it there.

A glimmer of hope shot through me. It was small. I was no master of knives. But it was *something*. Having even a tiny defense bolstered my spirits.

Hurrying to keep up with Jolene, I took stock of where she was leading me. Not an airport. More like a hospital. Some kind of a health clinic. After passing empty hallways with no markings for directions, we came into a more open space. One by one, we passed rooms. Glass doors blocked most of them, but many had curtains hiding the people inside. Men and women, all in various forms of rest. Every patient had the works: IVs, wires leading to monitors, and charts of statistics.

It all seemed…normal. Like I was strolling through an ordinary hospital department.

“What is this?”

“The head labs,” Jolene answered.

Right. Nothing *normal* about this. It should have been. It could have been. If Scott lived and he and Rosa could lead their team, this place could have existed as a hub of medical miracles. That original dream for a cure to cancer was a nightmare instead.

“Is this where all the torture happens?”

Jolene ceased walking. She spun in a slow pivot to face me, her perfect brows raised. As she tilted her head to the side, she crossed her arms. “Torture?”

She was going to play ignorant? I snorted. “Where you injure *patients* to see how far they can go before regenerating and living. Where they remove organs to see if *patients* can still live.”

Shaking her head, she smiled. Like I was a child missing a simple fact. “There is no torture in Project Xol. Only miracles. Gifts from the most talented woman on earth.”

I stepped forward. “How deluded are you?” I blinked, realizing she likely couldn’t even consider what I was saying. “There’s no talent in taking…” I huffed, recalling what Dale had explained to us, what Zero had dug up. “There’s no talent in taking babies to pump them with drugs to see how they react. There’s no gift in repeatedly pushing criminals to death only to draw them back.”

She lowered her arms, seeming more flustered. “You’ve got it wrong. What we do here is good. It’s a privilege.”

Someone passed around us in the wide hallway. The gurney went by first and I gasped at the sight of Ryan again. He was still lying there, shackled to the surface. His face was taut as he strained against something, his skin red, his eyes watering. A groan escaped his lips through clenched teeth.

"That's a privilege?" I snapped, pointing at the beast.

He jerked upright, his chest shaking.

Panting faster, freaked at the sight of him convulsing, I stepped back.

"One moment," Jolene politely asked of the person pushing Ryan by. The gurney stopped and Jolene gestured at him.

"A privilege. He's a perfect example of a man who's been blessed by Dr. Shaw's work."

Blessed? Did she hear herself? Blessed? Like he'd been treated with some reward by a goddess?

I spluttered, trying to find the simplest words to argue with her. "He— He...he's a murderer! He's supposed to be in prison. No. He's supposed to be dead for his crimes."

Jolene huffed. "Why should you care about who murders others when you've been screwing that…man you've been with."

She was *not* going there. Luke had killed because he had to, not because he'd wanted to. He'd done it to protect another. Kill or be killed. He wasn't anything like Ryan.

"Ryan isn't blessed to be alive because of Tami's manipulation. And it's no right of anyone on this team to play God and decide his life or death."

He groaned again and the agony of the sound hit me hard. I grimaced, watching his chest rise and fall in heaving gasps.

"How…did…" I swallowed hard. "How is he even here again?" I hated this man for trying to kill Luke, but I wasn't so cold to tune out his roars of pain. It cut me right down to the soul to witness another suffering, regardless of how horrible of a person they were.

Jolene grinned. "His body is meant to recover no matter the injuries sustained. He's one of the patients to have received the most advanced cure." She laid a hand on the rail of his bed, smiling at him like he wasn't jerking and in pain. "All of the advanced patients have trackers in them."

She faced me directly now, her face harder. "Dr. Shaw and Mr. Poole realized that when these advanced patients suffered bodily trauma, the commoners wouldn't know how to explain their recoveries. You know, like when fools shove others out of airplanes."

"Because he was trying to kill us!"

Rolling her eyes, she dismissed me. "No one would kill you. Not yet."

"Well, I sure feel special now."

"You're not. From what I can tell. Your beliefs are so…common, it's hard to think of you as her daughter."

Common. Like it was some insult? And they were, what? Xol elite?

"Dr. Shaw is… She's the most intelligent, generous person to exist."

"Only a sadistic psychopath would participate in unethical human experimentation."

She narrowed her eyes at me. "Haven't you ever heard of Machiavelli?"

"This is not the end to a means! It's torture. Haven't *you* ever heard of the Holocaust?"

Turning from me, she shook her head and started leading me further into the lab. "You don't even want to understand the beautiful, marvelous work that's happened here."

I fully comprehended what was going on. And more to the point, I was one against many of the same mind. Like a cult, these Xol freaks, if Jolene was any indication, were brainwashed to believe that they were doing something for the good. That they were the chosen ones to receive the cure to be abnormally regenerative and damn-near immortal. The praising tone and awed smile Jolene had when speaking about Tami—it was a show of reverence. No wonder she couldn't even consider how wrong all of this was.

"Right up here," Jolene said before a set of doors. Glass didn't make this entrance, and the idea of privacy beyond this way frightened me even more.

There wouldn't be a single person to help me here, but I did not want to face my biological mother alone.

Still, I held my head high and entered the room. Jolene smirked at me and gestured at a chair. We were the only ones there, as the guards who'd trailed us remained in the hallway. Besides the standard waiting-room style seat I had, there was a counter with a blank computer screen, an exam table, and a stool. In any other circumstances, it would have looked exactly like a real doctor's exam room.

One difference was the depth. More space was cordoned by a curtain and I shivered to think of someone else back there.

"Is she here?" I heard a woman say from the hallway.

"Yes, Dr. Shaw," Jolene said, making room for someone to enter. Her posture straightened like a soldier would for a commander. "She's right here."

"About time," Dr. Tami Shaw snapped as she strode in. With a sure gait, she moved with the speed and practicality of a woman who likely didn't waste her breath on anything beneath her esteem.

Which, with the way she narrowed her sharp gaze on me and curled her lips into the start of scowl, seemed to be me.

She doesn't like what she sees? I mocked a grin. "Never is too soon to give you the time of my day."

She straightened from studying me and I quickly noticed the similarities. I didn't doubt she'd conceived me. We shared the same blue eyes, hers a little darker. Our chins carried identical points and her cheeks were high like mine. After assuming so many false ideas, and after learning of deceptive lies, I was facing my biological mother. The woman who'd birthed me.

"Has she been like this the whole time?" Her words were twisted uglier by the wince on her flawless face.

Jolene scoffed. "She's very…"

I finished it for Jolene. "Common. Yeah. I'm as ordinary as you'll get." And I was damn proud of my difference to these people.

"She's been out for the majority of the day," someone else said.

Tami stepped to the side and I watched as Michael stood closer. “She remained unconscious during the chopper and plane flights.” He shrugged peering at me.

Helicopter and *plane? How long was I asleep? Hours?* So much time had passed since I’d been gone from Luke. Worry for him spiked.

Still staring at me, Tami paced a bit back and forth.

I could only take so much of the scrutiny, this awful, trapping sensation of being something like an object for them to appraise. “Don’t like what you see?”

She had yet to lose that disapproving expression.

I huffed. “No surprise. You clearly didn’t like me when I was a baby either. Maybe you *can’t* teach an old dog new trick—”

She backhanded me. My face flung back like I’d been assaulted by a two-by-four.

Sucking in a deep breath, I willed my eyes to remain dry. *God damn, does she pack a punch.* With my hands still cuffed, I raised them to touch my tender skin. Tasting blood, I swallowed hard. *Punch. Slap. Whatever.* My biological mother resorting to physical abuse on our first reunion spoke volumes.

I wouldn't give her the satisfaction of my pain. Lowering my hands to my lap, I straightened in my seat and faced her. I licked my split lip and met her gaze.

She stood there with her hands in her white lab coat, one foot away from her stance, jutting a hip out. So…indifferent. "No, I've never liked what I saw in you—there was no reason to. But I'd needed you. I slept with Scott to persuade him to agree to my research goals. Anything to distract him from listening to Rosa's nonstop caution." She huffed. "You only exist because I needed an in with your father."

My breaths flared from my nostrils. I didn't trust myself to open my mouth. Hatred spread through me like a disease, torching my every thought. Hearing her so callously dismiss me, like I didn't matter at all except to be her pawn.

"And now you'll be of use once more." She tore her disdainful regard from me and went to the countertop. She tapped at the monitor to wake up the screen as she asked Michael, "Do you have the vial?"

"No."

As soon as the man spoke, Tami pounded her fist to the metal countertop. The surface dented in several inches, creating a deep V for a pencil to roll toward and fall. Her *hand* had done that. Like a sledgehammer might. I slowly released the breath I'd sucked in, realizing she'd gone easy on striking me. With her display of super force, I had to accept an uglier fact. Tami wasn't just the mastermind of keeping Project Xol alive, she'd given herself the cure.

"Where is it?" she seethed.

"One of my agents took it. He hasn't reported in yet."

Tami set her hands on the edge of the counter, her shoulder blades rising up under her coat. Each deep breath she claimed, tension rose. Michael frowned, watching her back. “I have a man on it. It won’t take long for him to report in.”

“See that he does,” Tami snapped at him.

I smiled now, ignoring the blood dribbling on my shirt. “You do know it won’t last.”

Tami whirled to glower at me.

“Don’t you?” I said, taking pleasure in egging her on. Anything to piss her off.

“It’s been frozen,” Michael said.

“*Was*,” I argued. “Until someone broke in. The case it’s in right now will protect it for up to forty-eight hours, minus the time since you left.”

Tami turned her scornful stare to him.

He held his hands up, like placating a predator. “We’ve been over this, Tam.”

Tam? Just who the hell was he to her? Michael was the first Xol patient. And now…he was something of her equal?

My breath hitched as I stared at him. The last time I’d seen him, he’d been pinned under Luke, taking punch after punch in the face. There was no mark of any physical injury on his square jaw and clear flesh. So, if he was *here*, what happened to Luke?

He can't be dead. He can't be. We'd only just met in the most unexpected chances. Our connection germinated in bizarre extremes of reality. We'd had mutual grounding with lust, but our chemistry had grown into something infallible. Our love could not have been snuffed by this man's hands.

He would have brought Luke here, anyway. If Michael had Luke, he'd likely want to use him as leverage for my cooperation.

Please, please let him be safe somewhere far away.

"We don't need that vial." He pointed at me. "She's got Scott's data. We can identify the beta subspecies and get new DNA to use."

"That will take too long!" Tami lashed out at him, fists clenched and face turning pink. "I've already waited too long for this."

"It's our next best option. We have the code, and we'll be able to find the natives we need—wherever they are in that lake."

I shook my head. "Not without knowing the lake's setup." I smiled at him. "And you killed the woman who could show you."

Tami barked a laugh. "The refuge woman? Casal? Ramon Casal's daughter?"

"Yeah. Elena was stabbed by one of your freaks. Seems you shot yourself in the foot there." I gloated on this small victory. I wasn't sure if they could figure out Elena's setup of which natives were in which net in the lakes. But the longer I could keep any Xol members away from Xochimilco, the better. At least until the vial was destroyed.

"You might be misguided on the concept of *death*," Tami taunted. She held up a hand, silencing Michael from saying whatever he'd opened his mouth for. "However, it's past time I have Scott's data." She zeroed her dark gaze on me and said, "Give it to me."

I flipped her off.

Michael shook his head and growled as he reached to his pocket. Another syringe. Great. Time for la-la land again. Michael was the first Xol patient, but it seemed he played the role of an obsessively drug-happy security guy now.

"No." Tami put her hand to his chest and he stopped advancing toward me. "She won't be able to give it to me when she's unconscious."

"I won't give anything to you, ever."

"It sickens me that my offspring can be so naïve."

She could insult me left and right and it wouldn't sway me in her favor. Besides— "And what good would my father's data do? His is only half of it."

"For as much of a pain in the ass you are, I assume you're capable of simple math," Tami retorted. "One plus one *does* equal two." She slow clapped. "We already have the other half."

I frowned, fearing what she'd say next. Because if she had Rosa's half of the data—and Hendrick had died with his in his head—that meant Michael probably hadn't been bluffing.

No. Is Rosa...here? My heart raced faster.

"Maybe you'll reconsider your cooperation with an incentive. I'll dumb it down as much as I can. You give me the data until that vial shows up." She strode toward the curtain and gripped it. "Or you can watch Rosa die."

CHAPTER FOUR
LUKE

I had no way to be sure, but I was surrounded.

It has to be them.

People were everywhere. Going from the mountainside to Elena's refuge, and now to a bustling metropolis, I was overwhelmed at the crowds. Or maybe it was the effect of being on the run for so long with Cassidy. Staying off the grid and keeping a low-key existence primed me to be agoraphobic.

But I wasn't about to ignore my gut instincts. They'd served me well on the streets, in prison, and in every moment since I'd found Cassidy. And they were telling me that Xol mutants were covering the airport. There wasn't a uniform or identifying tag to mark them. I could only base my observations on what I'd experienced.

Muscles beyond even the most tripped-up steroid user. Stern, unflinchingly hostile expressions. The way a few of them—people who should have been strangers—tracked me with their stares.

I'd parked the van and entered the terminal an hour ago. Zero hadn't answered my call, and so I waited. I knew he knew what I needed to do. Or what he needed to get me. A location on Cassidy. A ticket purchased…somehow. Zero was the hold-up, and so I stalled. Back and forth, I strolled the terminal, careful not to pull attention to my nervous walking.

So far, I hid it well. Travelers came and went, no one paying me mind as I waited far longer than I wanted to. Except those freakish people who more than once glanced my way.

If any Xol mutants were poised up ahead, waiting for me to fully enter the airport after checking in at an airline, I needed to be able to move fast and evade them.

Tramer's cell buzzed in my pocket and I whooshed out a deep breath. "Zero," I answered so he'd know it was me again. "Where is she?"

"Just texted you the site. It's outside LA."

"What's there?"

Zero's end went choppy but he repeated the garbled bit. "I think a lab."

"Okay."

"I need to figure out a flight for you." Again, more static.

"I can't hear you," I said.

"I need to figure out a flight for you. I've been checking surveillance at where I believe the plane landed, but it's kicking me out. They got their shit covered."

Zero admitting he'd met his match? I refused to believe this hacker could fail.

"And I think Tramer's trying to reach me. Dammit." He growled. "I can't— I gotta— I gotta answer this. Sit tight, and I'll get back with a flight for you."

He hung up and I frowned, absentmindedly watching the pedestrian traffic go by. Tramer? Relief hit me at the knowledge Tramer had to be alive to attempt contacting Zero. Unless it was a ploy, the Xol using Tramer for intel.

No. I couldn't be that pessimistic. Nor could I be this patient.

Cassidy had been taken… I looked at the clock near a billboard kiosk. She'd been taken two hours ago. I didn't want to think of what could have happened to her.

I'm… I tapped the cell phone to my thigh, torn at being stuck here and unable to get her back. *I'm coming for you, baby. I am.*

Zero was busy, though, and it wasn't for something trivial. If he could get a hold of Tramer, we might know more of what happened to that coveted vial of DNA. If Tramer had retrieved it, then we could use that as leverage to get Cassidy back. And even if the vial was lost or destroyed, we could still bluff that we had it, if Tramer had taken care of the Xol mutant who'd snatched it.

Tramer was retired from the very business of dangerous hostage situations and more. He'd know how to phrase this plan. Which meant I needed Zero to find him, suggesting that I was on my own for the time being, waiting for a flight to be arranged.

Dammit. Stalling wasn't my thing. Waiting was my pet peeve. But what else could I do? I was out of people.

Or not... I'd never been solo in life, not really. Even thinking about the one person whose number I knew by heart had me cringing.

Jonah? My baby brother?

I rubbed at my face and checked another glance at the pair of beefy, men with stony glares. They'd been standing there by the vending machines, not moving from their post, and I caught them watching me red-handed. They had way too much interest in me for it to be a coincidence.

Jonah? I didn't want to bring him into danger. I'd killed to keep him safe. I'd spent years in prison to ensure his wellbeing.

But…I had to. We weren't teens or even young adults anymore. Jonah wasn't the idiot kid who'd drank too much and thought with his dick instead of his brain. He'd been sober and healthy—probably the strongest he'd ever been since he'd opened his gym business.

My only relative wasn't a weak guy to consider for help. Calling him for assistance depended only on my hesitation to bring him into this. For so long, I'd stuck to my decision to spare him any involvement in this Xol mess.

I have to. Because if I didn't call Jonah and something happened to Cassidy while I took too long to reach her, I'd never be able to live with myself.

I sucked in a deep breath and dialed his number.

"Hello," Jonah answered curtly. Suspiciously, even. Wind sounded in the background.

"It's me."

"Luke!" He sighed. "It's Luke."

Who's he talking to?

"Yeah. It's him." Then to me, "Dale's with me. He's been hiding out with me since he got shot. Doesn't want his company to know where he is since he had that mole in his office."

I scowled. Jolene. Yeah, I hadn't forgotten about her. From my peripheral vision, I glanced at the men I suspected were Xol mutants. They hadn't taken their sights from me yet.

"And he's been telling me about it. All this bullshit. The regenerative lizards. And the prison guys. And experimenting on all kinds of people."

I let him rush out the ramble. Learning about this top-secret mad scientist crap hit you like that. A whirl of too much bad news.

"They're salamanders, actual—"

"Whatever the hell they are! Where are you?" he asked.

"Mexico City."

"Mex—"

"I need your help."

Jonah didn't hesitate. "Anything."

I closed my eyes for a second, hating his eagerness to help. *If anything happens to him...* I opened my eyes and frowned. Well, then what? I had two options, consider Cassidy being hurt, or Jonah. Both of them mattered to me. And Jonah coming along had to be an asset, not a hindrance. I had to stop thinking of him as the younger version of him. Most importantly, I had to let go of this control. The need to always take charge and handle it all.

Just...lean on him. For once.

"I need you to help me get Cassidy back."

"Your girl? She was taken?"

I sighed, hating the reality of my words. "Yeah. To LA. I need a flight."

"We'll handle it." Then he spoke fainter, likely talking to Dale. "We need to fly him to LA." Back to me, he said, "He's gotta have a plane or something somewhere. We'll get you there."

"Without attracting trouble…"

"Of course. And don't think for a second you're going alone, you stubborn asshole."

I ran my hand through my hair. "Thank you."

"Can I call you back at this number? Dale's already making calls."

"Yeah."

"Ten minutes, tops." And he hung up.

The next time the cell rang, though, wasn't in ten minutes. Just after I hung up with Jonah, it buzzed.

Zero?

The screen showed his *Star Trek* alias. A text.

T-man's alive. Working on location.

I would let him have at it. The faster he connected us, the better. I replied that I'd secured a flight myself and he gave a thumbs up to that.

When Jonah called back, he provided instructions to check-in for Dale's private jet that would be flown to the airport immediately. I couldn't expect everything to fall in place as quickly as I'd like, but each minute until it was time to go passed by slowly.

I'm coming, baby. I'll never give up on you.

Before I could simmer into more of a nervous wreck waiting, it was time to move. Check-in went smoothly, and to my fortune, I didn't need to pass through the bulk of the foot traffic. Instead of heading toward the commercial terminals, where I suspected Xol mutants waited for me, an employee escorted me all the way to Dale's private aircraft.

In any other circumstances, I would have taken the time to notice and appreciate the luxury I was lucky to experience. Nerves and dread twisted into a steady weight as we prepared to take off, and I sat there edgy and bouncing my knee during the entire flight.

Jonah had said he and Dale would meet me at the airport within an hour of my arrival, and true to his word, I was soon reunited with my sibling.

"God *damn*, is it good to see you," Jonah said as he crushed me into a hug. I was taller and larger, but I struggled for a decent breath as he bear-hugged me.

I returned the gesture. "Thanks for com—"

He patted me hard on my back as he released me.

I flinched, feeling the soreness of all the fights I'd been in since…God, forever, it seemed. He frowned at me and said. "You helped me go after my girl before. Now it's my turn to help you. No more of this mushy gratitude crap."

No more emotional stuff? Fine by me. Just the same, I admired the hell out of the honorable man my brother had become. I suspected he'd always suffered guilt—for me covering his ass when trouble came with his girlfriend. He'd never come out and said it, but it wasn't hard to guess Jonah could be carrying the burden of thinking he was to blame for my time in prison. Indirectly, maybe he was. But I'd made *my* choices, and I'd act to defend him in a heartbeat again.

"Dale," I said, offering my hand to the older CEO to shake.

He shook it and nodded once. "Let's get out of here to discuss what needs to be done."

What needed to be done? Simple. Get Cassidy and stop Project Xol, however we could.

Ending the research—which felt like too kind of a word for grotesque human manipulation—was exactly what we spoke about. Once we'd left the airport, Jonah drove a rental to a hotel. In a suite, we decided what we could do.

It was an immense help that Dale had slowly but thoroughly explained everything to Jonah. The men had been moving around from hotel to hotel, after Dale realized his offices weren't safe places to carry on with delicate calls.

"I've already been reaching out," he said as I practically inhaled the takeout we'd had delivered. I hadn't thought I'd be able to stomach anything, but Jonah roughly scolded me to just eat something, for strength. At the first whiff of greasy noodles and spiced meat, my body told me what was needed.

"To who?" I asked around the food in my mouth. This was too urgent of a matter to bother with manners.

Jonah opened his mouth to speak but closed it before he lost his food.

"A couple of congressmen. New faces to the political arena. But they're openminded enough to hear me out," Dale said. "*Without* the expectation of campaign donations."

Done scarfing his bite down, Jonah wiped at his chin and added, “And the foreigners.”

Dale nodded. “A select few servicemen in Interpol.”

I swallowed my food down too early and coughed. “Not the FBI? CIA?”

The owner of Daysun shook his head. “I’ve already been aware of Xol presence and manipulation in our Armed Forces. My contacts overseas aren’t as…”

“Bought?” Jonah suggested. “Pushed over and corrupted?”

“Some of them are,” Dale argued, “but I’m careful who I align with.”

I trusted his judgment even if I wasn’t quite following his strategy. “How are a few foreign agents going to have jurisdiction here? And how could a couple low-ranking congressmen stop anything?”

Jonah held up a finger as he gulped some water down. Dale beat him to speaking. “It will be a doubled-up approach. I have the means to buy out labs. Maybe not *every* facility the entire Project has in use right now. I can purchase the majority of what is on our land, and vetted business associates can probably be encouraged to take care of buying out the international branches of Xol."

I laughed once. "Buy out? I don't think Tami's going to be putting anything up for sale." And if he could have done that, why hadn't he already?

Jonah said, "She won't have a choice when we expose the truth."

"We'll leak it all to the press." Dale smirked. "I have more than enough members of the press to contact."

"We'll be whistleblowers to the entire Project?" I asked. I ignored my food long enough to watch Dale. He didn't avoid my attention and met my stare head-on. At first, when I'd learned that Daysun was the original funder for Project Xol, way back when Cassidy's father and Rosa were at the helm of the research, I'd suspected this billionaire of being an accomplice to it all. Yet as he'd explained his role of ending his funding while keeping an eye on the project from a distance, I'd learned he truly cared about this nightmare. He'd more than proven he'd valued Jonah's and my lives, since he'd intervened and saved my life twice. It was almost ironic that the man who'd been critical to spearheading the research was now the guy who was scheming to bring it all down.

A full circle, indeed.

Jonah nodded as Dale said, "As soon as I can gather a cohesive trail of documents as proof, the media's going to bite."

"They'll bite and shit will hit the fan," Jonah said. "Mutated humans discovering and hiding a cure to cancer? People manipulating the government? Testing on people?" He huffed. "It'll spread like this." He ended with a snap of his fingers.

"It'll require…" Dale leaned back into his chair and rubbed at his closed eyes. He blinked them open and sighed. "For something of this magnitude, it'll take me some time to gather the proof. I can't trust anyone in my office to handle seeking out the documents. That's why it's been so hard to ever think about ending the Project. They hide everything behind governments they can bribe for secrecy. Tami is elusive."

Proof of what Project Xol had warped into? Well, I could get that.

"I've got someone who's more than familiar with proof." I pulled out my phone and texted Zero. "He's been helping us all along. Cassidy's friend and a world-class hacker." As I waited for Zero to reply, I eyed both men. "But what are we going to do about getting Cassidy out of their lab?"

"Easy." Jonah stood and set his hands on his hips. "We're gonna show up and make them give her back."

Easy. Yeah, right.

CHAPTER FIVE

CASSIDY

I shot to my feet as soon as I saw Rosa.

She sat there on a stiff-looking chair, her arms and legs strapped to the metal, a tube of liquid delivering something from an IV bag. Her frizzy graying hair hung in a haphazard mess yet still stuck up at odd ends. Normally tan, she was pale, wan, with too many wrinkles easy to follow like etchings on her typically serene and serious face. She instantly captured my gaze, her dark eyes alert and cautious.

I didn't get more than two feet toward her when Michael hauled me back to my chair. I wriggled, fighting his grip, desperate to reach my true parent and yank that damn IV from her.

"Do not sedate her," Tami warned as she strode into the room.

Michael growled as I resisted him shoving me to the chair. "Jolene. Get the straps." He came around to stand behind the chair, giving me another chance to see Rosa. She licked her dry lips and I studied her again.

How dare they drug her and give her such a sallow pallor.

How dare they hurt her and give her that black eye and gash on her lip.

How dare they—

I cried out a groan as Michael gripped my biceps and squeezed hard. His fingers were like tentacles of steel, his strength inhuman.

"Easy," Rosa said, her voice cracked and tired.

I stilled. She tilted her head slightly, a subtle show of authority. It was a small tick, a tell. Something she'd always done when disciplining me. A tiny cue not to mess with her request.

Jolene came closer and unlocked my handcuffs. Together, she and Michael strapped me to the chair just as Rosa was.

I huffed out a hard breath and narrowed my eyes at Rosa. Okay. Easy? She wanted me to calm down? I'd give her that. For now. The thick material locking my limbs to this hard chair promised I would have no freedom to do my will. I could chill for her if it'd help.

"I see you've tamed the brat. Even if she's a disrespectful fool," Tami said, "she *can* be obedient."

Studying the IV bag and the line into Rosa's arm, I snapped at her. "You're wasting your time if you think I'll obey *you*. I will never help you destroy humanity."

"Destroy humanity. Do you have to be so dramatic?" Tami gave a long-suffering sigh. "Give me the data."

"Don't," Rosa said.

I didn't intend to, but if I could stall, until I could figure out a way to get Rosa from whatever was in that IV…

I heaved out an exasperated breath. “I don’t even have it anymore.”

“You do,” Michael insisted.

Technically, I did, in a way. Zero had the data electronically, and there was no way I’d give him up. I shook my head. Like they’d know I copied those files.

“Don’t play games,” Tami said.

“I. Don’t. Have. The. Data.” *On me…*

“That’s not what she said.” Tami stomped over past Rosa.

What who said?

I hadn’t even glanced around the room, assuming it was identical to the divided space I’d first been brought to. Now, I saw that we weren’t alone. Further from me and Rosa strapped to chairs and facing each other was someone else. Lying on a hospital bed was Elena.

She’s alive? When I’d run off, she’d been prostrate on the ground, feet from the lake’s edge. A knife had been driven into her chest, likely her heart, and she *still* lived? I blinked, not trusting my vision.

"I…I told them," Elena admitted, defeat in her every breath. "I told them you said you had them." Her eyes belied her guilt.

Dammit. I pursed my lips. "She said she said," I quipped. Facing Tami, I repeated. "I don't have the data."

"They…they…" Elena struggled to sit up but couldn't get far. Her face twisted and she slumped back to the mattress with a whoosh. "They were going to kill Rosa if I didn't talk."

She'd betrayed me, telling Tami whatever she'd likely asked. I couldn't make the connection between how adamantly Elena had schemed to destroy further chances of using axolotls for unethical science and now how quickly she'd surrendered here. At the sake of saving Rosa, I understood her choice. But…I couldn't dismiss the fleeting stab of her letting me down. This abrasive woman who'd judged me from the moment she met me. She'd given in to them.

"You were dead," I said instead, still struggling to bridge the gap of details in my mind.

"She was *dying*," Tami corrected.

You might be misguided on the concept of death. I picked at Tami's words, fitting the pieces in to seeing Elena very much alive and able to share secrets with the enemy.

"She was dying but not yet gone," Tami repeated. "So we gave her a specific type of the cure." She crossed her arms and regarded Elena like she was admiring her handiwork. "We nicknamed this strain of the cure Last Time. The Xol cure is typically built up over a succession of doses, to prepare for accepting the genetic mutations throughout the whole body. Regeneration is a complicated series of changes, and it can be taxing on the human physique. Last Time is faster, stronger, replacing the process of a year's worth of normal doses. It's a speedier procedure to rapidly regenerate a dying patient."

I remained silent, unable to accept this one woman deciding fates like it was her right.

"I see you have no words. It can be unbelievable at first. To think we can pull someone back from dying. To save those who don't want to go. I know

Rosa's probably trained you into thinking I'm so mal—"

I snarled at her. "She never found you worthy of mentioning."

Tami's nostrils flared. "Regardless, don't be so simple-minded and quick to judge the amazing work we do here, like saving lives."

Amazing? I recalled the macabre convulsions that Ryan rode out as he was brought back here. The agony and pain he beseeched me with in his soulless gaze.

"Amazing, my ass." Elena ground out the words before she, too, reacted to strain against her bonds. Groaning, she jerked and flopped, her teeth smashed together and her eyes squinted shut. Her scream rent the air and Tami sighed.

"Jolene, let's move her back to her room. She's crashing again."

Crashing? Like really dying?

"Amazing?" Elena spat out. She screamed. "This hell is worse than death itself!"

Michael and Jolene went to her bed and began pushing her to the exit.

Tami turned toward us. "I'll let you two have a moment together." She checked her watch and pointed at Rosa's arm. "Because she only has hours left until the drugs she's receiving poison her beyond hope." As she went to the door, she paused and looked back. "And Rosa, you definitely wouldn't be privileged enough to get the Last Time and have a second chance at your pathetic life."

Once the door shut, I whipped back to take in Rosa's rough appearance again. Before I could launch into an inquisition, I had to shake the images of Elena seeming to struggle crawling out of her skin. I'd never been a fan of scary movies, but that was like watching a demonic possession in real time. "What's happening to her?"

"There's so much you don't know." She began and shook her head. The sadness in her tone was unwarranted. She wasn't patronizing me in her superior scientific know-how. There was no way she could understand how much I *did* know.

"Dale Hanson got in touch with me back at…" Jesus. Trying to explain the hell I'd gone through and the locations I'd traveled since her first letter would take too long. I wasn't sure what Tami meant by "giving us a minute." The woman was so domineering, she probably thought she called time by her standards. "He's been following the events since your apartment was bombed. And he caught up with me—and explained *a lot*."

"Dale." She pursed her lips. "He's been following much more than that for even longer. He was always keeping abreast of the Project. Hendrick stayed in touch with him and it was through their friendship that we were loosely aware of what Tami has been doing all this time."

"Hendrick…" I inhaled a deep breath.

Her eyes watered as she stared at me, waiting for me to say more, but then she nodded, clamping her lips shut tighter. "I always knew… I always knew they'd catch up to him."

"They did, and didn't. He was caught by the cartel and they thought he was competition."

Rosa took a shaky breath and cleared her throat. "I never wanted anything to do with it. After Tami slept with Scott and began tainting him with her quest for power, I knew there would be no good end to this. That greed for the success…that was what frightened me the most."

"So you left."

She frowned. "I did. Your father and I fell fast for each other, but ours wasn't a love that could last. When I learned that he'd cheated on me with Tami, and when you were born, I stood by him. He was my husband, and I was fond of him."

She shook her head, pursing her lips. "But we were discussing divorce. I wanted out of the Project and he wanted me to continue—with the research, if not him. I couldn't stand it, her or the fear of the trials she wanted. After the lab was destroyed in Nottingham, Hendrick and I changed our research goals and I adopted you."

"Why was the lab destroyed?"

She huffed. "Tami. She staged it all so she could start anew as the true leader. As time passed, people talked. Colleagues and researchers heard rumors of such world-changing medical experiments. Word spread that pharmaceutical companies were paying for something big. Others bragged about their 'donations' to fund it. We suspected Tami was alive, not dead as reported. I told Hendrick to let things lie, but he couldn't let it go. He felt responsible for it, somehow. We were all members of a team but he felt even his participation—all of us—had given Tami the opening to begin this horror."

I couldn't speak, hearing her reasoning behind the crisis change of her life. Hating that she'd wanted a life away from all of this.

"I never wanted you to know."

Now it was my turn to huff. "Well, that letter sure said otherwise."

She swallowed and nodded gravely. "I'm sorry. I…I had no other choice."

"Why did you ask me to help?" I wasn't mad that I'd gotten involved, but I was nobody in the grand realm of medical science. What had she really expected?

"I couldn't trust anyone else. I asked former grad students to mail those letters for me, I was so scared of even those being traced. Over the last few months, Hendrick and I noticed attempts to steal our academic files from various locations where we'd worked over our careers. One by one, all of our former labs and facilities were breached—data was stolen. We kept our most sensitive data close to us, but Scott had already stored his data before he was killed. The library in Texas was the last location they'd yet to go for the data, and I'd hoped to beat them to it. And…I needed to hide you. What better way to stay out of sight by staying on the move?"

"Hide me from…Tami?"

She nodded.

You're needed again. What did my biological mother want to use me for now? I couldn't ask before Rosa continued. She glanced at the door, perhaps nervous we'd run out of time to speak privately.

"I never changed your name after the lab was ruined because I'd believed they were both dead. Scott, I *knew* he was gone—I had to identify his remains. Tami was declared dead as well. When you were four, Hendrick said Dale had caught word she was seeking funding for research, that she'd been behind the destruction of that first lab. She'd never expressed any joy or desire for motherhood, when she was pregnant or when you were born, but still, I feared she'd come to get you."

I shook my head. "Why? She hadn't wanted me for those four years."

Rosa almost smiled at me. "I…I don't know. It was a fear nonetheless. I'd grown so attached to you. It never occurred to me *not* to adopt you. Even though I'd married Scott foolishly, he *was* my family. He loved you despite how you were conceived, and I couldn't help but love you as well. You were the child I never could have had and I was desperate to keep you safe. Even from a distance. I hoped you'd be safest at schools away from me, to prevent her from getting to you through me."

Her words soothed a buried ache in my heart. She'd pushed me away for my safety—even if Tami had never shown any interest in having me in her life.

Not because Rosa hadn't wanted me. But to protect me.

"And here I am now. Why?"

"I'm not entirely sure, but I have my guesses. If they wanted to turn you into one of those mutants, they would have already."

I agreed, thinking over what we might be missing.

Rosa expelled a deep breath. "Like I said, we'd stayed abreast of the Project through Dale. There was never any way to fight back, to tell the world about it with how far their reach went, but we refused to claim ignorance. The latest discoveries he'd shared with us were of that Last Time she just spoke of."

"The cure that pulls people back from the dead."

Rosa nearly smirked, brightness coming to her sad eyes for a moment. "They're not…zombies."

I grinned. She'd *never* cared for anything paranormal or sci-fi in the reaches of fiction. She was too strongly rooted in what life was capable of in reality. Only, we were damn near living the essence of farfetched truths. "The Xol freaks? I'd say they're more like vampires. Regenerating and healing over."

She lost the fraction of mirth as I quickly asked, "What's happening to Elena?"

"They gave her the Last Time to keep her alive for answers. Regeneration is not a process that should be expedited. It takes time. Cells need to reproduce rapidly and that requires enormous energy. It's not like a switch. As she said, doses usually are increased over time, probably to achieve a rate of the body mutating in a steady balance. Too much of the cure too fast can overwhelm the person."

"How?"

Rosa shifted in her seat. "When regenerative mutations get to the endocrine system, the reaction becomes uncontrollable. The production of hormones is skewered."

I nodded. Zero had mentioned this before in one of our calls. He'd referenced test analyses of the patients developing hormonal complications—growing angrier, moody with unreliable mental states.

"If the process is introduced too fast, as they do with the Last Time dose, the change can drive the person insane. We'd heard of patients going berserk, killing the techs, doctors, and staff when the doses are administered. Even killing themselves—if they can."

I closed my eyes. Shooting up people on their deathbed with liquid insanity. Tami truly had no bounds.

"They'd worked to equilibrate these cases. But it's not perfected, as you can see with Elena. The psychoactive changes had been targeted, but not the inflammation. As cells reproduce rapidly, as organs are duplicated, bones rebuilt…it comes with inflammation. I cannot even imagine the pain of having your organs doubled and destroyed from the inside out."

I shuddered, wishing I could erase that knowledge from my mind. It sounded right, though. Inflammation throughout the body. Just like what Elena had looked like, fighting an inferno within her skin.

"And that's their newest advancement? This Last Time?" I asked.

"That was what Dale had been finding."

All right… Then what about it? Clearly, they were utilizing the drug. It didn't have anything to do with me specifically. I couldn't shake the feeling I wasn't here simply for giving them Scott's data. And if they wanted to test out the Last Time on me, they'd been too careful *not* to kill me.

Frowning, I studied Rosa again.

"They have my half of the code," she admitted with a long face. "They'd captured me the day after I'd called you. I fell for their bluff, that they'd found you." She sniffed. "It… It was just some girl. They'd beaten her face, but her shape and size, even her hair. I could have sworn it was you. As they…" She closed her eyes for a moment. "As they removed…"

I cringed, hating I couldn't hug her. Anything to reassure her I was okay. Something to erase the awful things she'd witnessed. "Removed…?" I swallowed around the lump in my throat.

"Parts of her…" She sat up straighter and blanked her face. "They tortured her in front of me and I cracked. I gave them my half of the code only for them to kill her. For three days they'd left me in a room with her corpse and it was only when they'd removed her body that they told me they'd located you."

All that time she'd been trapped with what she thought was me.

"Rosa…" I sobbed once and hated the tears that burned down my cheeks.

"I've been here for…a week?" She frowned, as though she was trying to concentrate. "Or more."

"And you're leaving today."

She raised her brows. "Not much point if I'm no longer alive." Lifting her hand almost in a wave, she brought my attention back to her arm hooked to the poison.

"What is it in there?"

"They wouldn't explain. Something to weaken me, to slow my cardiovascular strength."

"Is there an antidote?"

She shrugged. "I'm not sure. It doesn't matter. All we can decide and do now is to take this fight to the grave. Or I will. They tricked my code from me but—"

"I'm not giving her anything, Rosa."

"You better not. Even at the risk of losing me."

Jesus. Don't say that. There has to be…a loophole. Another way out of this. I couldn't lose her too.

"You're too expressive to hide your feelings, Cassidy. I know what you're thinking. Do not risk saving me to beat her. You cannot let her get a hold of the beta subspecies. She cannot have Scott's code to get them."

"Why? What's so special about that beta DNA?"

"They didn't show a statistically significant probability for the proclivity to acerbate unmanageable endocrine production."

I squinted. "In English?"

"They didn't cause hormonal problems."

I slowly nodded. "Okay…" So, what? Tami wanted to make nice mutants now? I bit back a snort.

"Fertility, Cassidy. Think of the hormones associated with fertility."

Fertility? Well, sure, there were lots of hormones in the reproductive end of life.

Oh. *Whoa.* I blinked at her. *Oh…no…*

"All the Xol patients are adults."

From what I saw, they were.

"Infants and children have been turned *into* Xols." Rosa licked her lips and simply said, "And now, I think there might be a chance she wants to *breed* them."

CHAPTER SIX
CASSIDY

Jolene returned to the room I shared with Rosa before we could speculate any more on what Tami was working on next—what she was hoping to do with the beta axolotl DNA. Or with me.

Breed? I refused to dwell on that particular panic. I'd never agree to be a baby farm for her freaks. They could kill me before they—

No. Wrong, Cass. They could *and likely will push me to death's edge, then pump me up with that Last Time crack, and* then *take what they wanted.*

I shivered and watched as Jolene backed up to the door and wheeled Elena into the room. She was asleep, or too drugged up to move.

"Dr. Shaw will be with you in a moment," Jolene said, too chipper for my mood.

For Rosa's either, it seemed, because she retorted, "Oh, stop calling her a *doctor*. She faked her death before she completed her thesis."

That Rosa was miffed Tami called herself a true graduate… I was sure I'd appreciate the humor another day. If I lived to see one.

"And she's not a *doctor* in any other sense. She's not here to help anyone be healthy," I said.

Jolene scowled at me. "When *Dr.* Shaw came to me and offered me a cure, do you know what I was? A weak, feeble failure of a human. My body betrayed me."

She was a cancer survivor, only she'd gotten her second chance at life with the accessories of unnatural strength, unpredictable emotions, and a warped sense of dedication to her rescuer.

"Now…" She splayed her hands at her perfect body. "Now I am *invincible.* All thanks to her genius."

"What about everyone else who's suffering from cancer?" Rosa challenged. "Or everyone else who's weakened by disease? If you can have your invincibility, why can't others? You have no right to pick and choose."

Jolene tossed a tired sigh to Rosa. "Because *every*one would want it. And not *every*one deserves it."

"Well, aren't you little Miss Hitler," I drawled. "Only *special* people can be made invincible. Let me guess, all the ones who aren't *special* enough are used for your experiments?"

"Those who sacrifice for the research of bettering us is only—"

"Inhumane!" Rosa roared.

"That's enough." Tami followed her words by striding into the room. "Jolene, if you can take Rosa to the next room, please."

"No." I jerked against my binds. "No!"

"Don't, Cassidy," Rosa said calmly as Jolene came to her chair.

Don't? If this was her version of a goodbye, telling me to not give in to Tami for the sake of saving her… Fuck. No. I wasn't going to let Rosa be a martyr.

It wasn't until Jolene tapped the toes of her high heels to the ends of Rosa's chair legs that I noticed the small wheels. With the brakes unlocked, my only family was taken from the room.

"Now. Without that judgmental old hag to interrupt us…" Tami rolled the stool closer to me and sat. "Where were we?"

"I don't know what you were doing but I was suffering through your puppet's vow for your so-called amazing science."

Tami halfheartedly smirked. "Jolene… I knew she was a keeper from the beginning. You see, sometimes it helps to condition patients with discipline."

I snorted. "Yeah. Like training them to be killers for your sick cause."

"Among other things. Security is a necessary branch of our goals. But we also implement what I like to call sublimation cleansing, so they can understand my team and I are their trusted source of guidance as their bodies adapt."

I mock gasped. "Oh. You mean, like, brainwashing."

She glowered. "Is it entertaining? To waste so much time on dramatics and sarcasm? Are you ever serious?"

"Like you give a shit what kind of a person I am."

Leaning back, she crossed her arms. "You're right. I don't."

I arched toward her, yelling, "Then why the *hell* am I here?"

She smiled. The coldness in her eyes mocked the curve of her lips. A cold spike of fear ran up my spine.

"Did Rosa ever tell you about your birth?"

Seriously? "No. Didn't you hear me the first time? She *never* felt you worthy of any mention."

Her smile dropped and it pleased me that insinuating she didn't matter was a jab. "When you were born, you destroyed me."

I laughed. And laughed. Until she slapped me. Harder than before. Crying with tears, I waited for my vision to clear. If you can't laugh, cry… Sitting upright once more, I still chuckled—maybe it was hysteria now—as I said, "I hate you."

"Oh, the feeling's mutual."

"I *destroyed* you? How poetic." She'd hated me on principle that much? Her having to carry me to life was so damn awful? Could she be any more selfish?

"Literally. Your placenta ruptured prematurely and I was taken for an emergency C-section. During that procedure, they'd found that my uterus had been damaged and they partially removed it."

"Bummer." I could not feel one speck of pity for this evil person.

She gritted her teeth. "It is unfortunate. It ruined my chances of having more offspring."

"Because you *love* kids so much."

Another slap.

"Only, it took me too many years to realize that wasn't the problem. Even in vitro yielded no births. That was when we'd started to focus on the hormonal differences of Xol patients."

"Ya fucked it all up, huh?"

"No. We just haven't perfected it yet. After trying several techniques, we went back to the original research, to find a solution to Xol infertility. And that's where we dug into those pieces of data about the beta DNA."

I wasn't surprised Rosa had guessed right. She had a brilliant mind. Tami *was* after the beta axolotl subspecies for procreation.

"My eggs are useless." She cocked her head to the side and peered at me. "But *yours* aren't."

I froze, feeling my face going slack. If I hadn't been grinding my teeth together at the atrocity of being in her presence, my jaw would have dropped. Blinking faster, I struggled to comprehend why she needed to declare that obvious comparison.

Too selfish to resist the temptation of invincibility and near immortality, she'd ruined her hormones and eggs. And mine were fine.

"You want me—"

"Jesus. I don't want *you.*"

Because she never had.

"I want your eggs."

Yeah. I had connected the dots right the first time. This deranged woman was really sitting here pointedly explaining she wanted my eggs. Like it was an ordinary request any woman might make to another. *Could I borrow a cup of flour, ma'am? No? How about I shop around your ovaries, then, hmm?*

I started to shake my head. How to reject her in the most irrefutable way…? "Fuck no." It came out on an incredulous laugh.

"Do you truly think you have a choice?"

I did. I sure as hell should. Unless she wanted to playact that she was some self-righteous dude in Congress, I *did* own the choice to do what *I* wanted with my body. In a normal world, that was how it should be. But here, I wasn't so cocky or deluded to think I could fight her. She could tranq me, cut me open, take my eggs, and dispose of me once again.

"Why me?"

She rolled her eyes. "You're my daughter."

"No, I'm not."

"In every biological sense of the word, yes, you are." She pointed at her chest. "*My* DNA is in yours. Whether you accept it or not, you are my bloodline."

Bloodline? What, was she going to start spouting about having a reign and some divine bullcrap next? "I don't care." I did, really. I'd rather be the child of literally any other woman on earth but I couldn't change the past.

"I care. You—your DNA—it's mine. It belongs to me."

Dear God. This freak was too far gone. What kind of a person assumes their kid is borrowing their genes?

She twisted one side of her lips up and drew a deep breath, like she was readying to lay down a lecture. "Jolene had a very valid point."

I rolled my eyes. Sure. Her brainwashed patient was only parroting Tami's points.

"If the Xol treatment were available to the world at large, do you know what would happen?" she asked.

"I bet anger management classes would spike."

She shook her head. "Everyone would want it."

Hardly. If everyone knew it'd trip you into a tweaked-out moody mess, many would opt out. That wasn't the point, though. No one should play God like that. If a true cure existed—without the craziness and manipulating lifespans, it shouldn't be hidden from the weak and vulnerable.

"If everyone could get their hands on it, then Xol recruits would be…common."

Two words stuck at me. *Recruits*, like she thought her patients were her minions and soldiers. And *common*. She pasted such a dirty edge to it.

"I haven't spent my life seeking this cure to let just anyone have it. This…" She stood abruptly, sending the stool crashing to the wall. "This cure is *mine*. I created it. I perfected it. Do you understand?"

That she had control problems? Definitely.

It must have been a rhetorical question because she paced and carried on. “Xol belongs to me, and those *I* deem worthy of it. *I* am the one who decides who should be saved. For years, I have arranged a specific formula for who can receive the treatment, but it is no longer enough. Because for every new recruit we save—”

“You’re not saving anyone! You’re making…an army of cult-like, nearly immortal freaks!”

She nodded, her expression still furiously serious. “True. I’ve been amassing recruits and followers as a baseline to my cause. Together, we will form a new human subspecies to rule over all else.”

Oh. My. God. She was unhinged. The Xol had more than fried her eggs. It had nuked her damn brain.

“In order to preserve a new and improved human subspecies, we must ensure they can procreate and carry on their genes.” She stopped pacing and faced me with her hands behind her back. “And I’m going to start in the most logical part. With myself, with my genes—in you. Because I will never forfeit this power."

CHAPTER SEVEN

LUKE

For hours, we strategized in the hotel room.

Zero had already given me the coordinates of the building he'd tracked Cassidy's plane arriving at. *Hours ago*. I rubbed at my face, loathing the wait of even one minute more. There was no telling what they might do to her. The unknown fear drained my concentration.

"Luke," Jonah said. He tapped at the map on the screen.

I shook my head and sat forward to pay attention.

He'd had his laptop with him and it was on there that we were plotting and testing our plan. The screen presented the blueprint of the facility that was otherwise regarded as a health clinic. We knew better. It had to be a mutant clinic if Project Xol operated it.

Across the room, Dale spoke on the phone with Zero. Since the moment I'd introduced the men, they'd been hashing out plans. What documents to send to which reporters. Which congressman could speak to which contact for assistance. How one Interpol officer could assist in which country. Arranging an internationally webbed whistleblower effort took a lot of talking and even more persuasion.

"Luke," Jonah said again, pulling me back from watching Dale pace, cell phone to his ear. "I know. You want to get Cassidy back. We will. But you gotta focus first."

I sighed and tipped a finger from my hands folded together. Pointing at Dale, I asked, "Do you think he can pull it off? Expose them?"

"Dale?" Jonah glanced at the man who'd mentored him through AA and beyond. "Of course." Then he raised his brows at me. "Can Zero?"

Zero had the easier end of it. In our phone call where I'd posed the solution of exposing Project Xol to the world, Zero had stated he had more than enough proof and evidence to share. It was more a matter of condensing it into something that could go viral and make sense to any ordinary citizen.

"Of course," I echoed.

"Then since *they* are handling their shit in this shitstorm we're brewing, how about *we* go over our roles again."

I scooted forward in my seat to study the screen again. His reassurance was more cockiness than confidence, but it had roused the fight in me. Dale and Zero could dismantle Project Xol by attacking them at their weakness. Confidentiality. Project Xol existed because it was top-secret, matters that were hushed by too corrupt rulers and businesses. Once we let the cat out of the bag, there would be no way they could continue.

Jonah's scold was legit. He and I had different tasks to complete, and if I let myself get distracted by worrying about Cassidy or loathing the surmounting odds against us, I'd be useless in rescuing her.

I'll have her in my arms tonight. And I'm never *letting her go.*

A month ago, a relationship was the last thing I'd even think about.

After meeting Cassidy, I was only glad I'd had a chance to experience the little I had with her.

No. No more of this. If they don't have the vial of beta DNA, then she should be safe. We'll have a future together. We'll have each other again. But only if I could concentrate now.

I nodded and followed along.

"Come *on*, man," Jonah groused, tapping at the screen. "We'll enter here…"

Jonah and I went through our place of breaching the Xol clinic. Posing as waste disposal employees, we'd enter the labs from the basement. We'd retraced our planned path over and over. Basement, to the kitchen, then up to the floor with patient rooms.

Borrowing my impromptu move in Mexico, we'd obtain uniforms of whatever kind they had to fit in. Then we'd get Cassidy, wherever she was being held. The one reassuring fact I clung to was that she had to be there. No other planes or vehicles had left the site. Unless they had underground transport, Cassidy was there.

Just as we ran through scenarios of thwarted escapes, singling out which exits might be easiest if it all went to hell, Dale waved us over.

"I'll put them on speaker," he said into his phone.

"Luke?"

It was Zero. "Right here."

"Good news or bad news?"

"Bad," Jonah said, butting in. At my glare, he shrugged. "That's the best way to go."

"Fine. Bad news?" I said.

Zero sighed a high-pitched noise. "The vial's gone."

I frowned. "Gone…how?" I brightened at even this so-called bad news, because if Zero knew this, it might mean he had to have been in touch with Tramer. Probably what the good news was.

"He didn't say. Just that it was gone. As in, he doesn't have it."

"Does the Xol patient have it?" Dale asked.

"He didn't say. It wasn't the best reception."

"Okay." I rolled my shoulders, relaxing a little more. If the vial was gone and the Xol couldn't obtain it, that had to be a plus for us. In the grand scheme of things, at least. Without that genetic material, Tami couldn't go forward with her next messed-up experiment. Dale had already told us about the most recent development from Xol labs, some kind of painful, insanity-inducing treatment to regenerate people near death. None of us knew what the vial's DNA could do for more developments, so with it out of the picture for now, nothing worse could happen.

Then again, I'd hoped to have that vial for an exchange in getting Cassidy back. A hostage negotiation of sorts.

"And the good news?" I asked.

"Uh. Just that Tramer's alive."

Yeah, I'd figured that one out. Too bad we couldn't have another small win. Regardless, I was glad he'd survived.

"Where is he?" I asked.

"Leaving Mexico. He's injured but he said he was getting out of there."

"To go where?" Jonah asked. "Here, with us?"

"He'd asked for Cassidy's location and I gave it to him. Kind of. The call ended before he could confirm it. And now, he's gotta be in the air."

Damn. We could use his help infiltrating the lab, but we couldn't wait for him. Our window was slim. Zero had found the waste disposal's schedule of pickups and the truck was scheduled to be there in two hours. None of us wanted to wait until the next pickup time—tomorrow evening.

It wasn't long before Dale drove me and Jonah to the waste disposal warehouse. Zero had already hacked into their computers. First, he'd canceled the order for pickup so no one on the staff would head out there. Then, he'd added us as employees with key passcodes to get into the building.

"Ready?" Dale asked as he set the rental in park. He glanced in the rearview mirror at each of us.

Ready? Memories of every time I'd asked Cassidy that came forth. And her hesitant, unsure but honest answer, usually a whispered *Fuck no.* Only, she wasn't that shy and nerve-wracked woman anymore. She'd adapted to the hell we'd been thrust into, rising as something even stronger. My badass woman. Whether or not she would have ever been ready for the events that followed Rosa's first letter, she *never* failed to try. And she did. Despite her fears or flaws, she tried her damn best.

Try a little longer, Cass. Just a little longer until I can help.

"Let's go," Jonah said with a nod.

I bobbed my head, too, reaching for the door handle. Apprehension of gearing up for a fight had me tense, but I leaned over to meet the reflection of Dale's gaze in the mirror. I gripped his shoulder in a pat. "Thank you."

He nodded. "Good luck."

Shit. We needed a lot more than luck. Besides, I'd probably depleted my lifetime's worth of it by successfully escaping the cartel.

No whining or wallowing. I exited the car on that hard advice and strode toward the warehouse with Jonah.

Jonah tapped in the number Zero had provided for us, and with the green dot blinking bright on the lockpad, we were in. No one was inside the large garage space. To the right was a small office. Lights were off. Made sense. It was the evening and the typical office staff were long gone. They must scale down the operations for their nighttime pickups.

In front of us was a fleet of large vans and trucks. Zero had the work order schedule of the Xol building's pickup details, so we were prepared to find the large truck with specific plates.

First, though, we went to the employee breakroom and found spare uniforms in a closet. Dressed in the company's gear, we checked that our guns were within easy reach underneath the fabric.

Disguised, we wove a path through the fleet of vehicles until we located the large truck that the pickup order stated.

"That's some big-ass wheels," Jonah quipped.

He'd always been the kind of guy to talk too much. As much as I knew he was probably using humor to reach me, I was too wired to reply and climbed up to the passenger seat. We'd already planned for Jonah to drive. Just in case security would check us at a gate. Just in case I might be recognized due to my association with Cassidy.

So far, everything was going to plan. With each successful step we passed, I wanted to believe. I wanted to bask in the confidence that I'd be celebrating a reunion with Cassidy tonight. Merely thinking of her, as I had so many times since she'd been flown from me, burned me with an ember of rage. If anything happened to her…

No. I fisted my hand and stared out the passenger window as Jonah pressed the garage door opener. *Don't go there. She'll be alive.* Fate couldn't be so cruel to take her from me when we'd hardly had each other to begin with.

The drive to the clinic was silent. Dread pooled heavy in the pit in my stomach and I concentrated on steady breaths to calm my too-fast heart rate. Anxiety could be good. Being revved up and alert would help keep me on my toes. Allowing my energy to morph into straight-out fear would spell disaster.

Don't think. No wallowing. Just do it and be done with it.

My pep talk stayed with me during the drive and it wasn't long before we pulled onto the drive to the facility. From a distance, there was nothing innocuous in its appearance. The professionally landscaped grounds and the clean, well-maintained exterior of the multistory building lacked any sense of foreboding. If I hadn't known what this place housed, I could have very well passed it in any city and assumed it was a legitimate business.

The lack of signage was the only clue that something might be fishy about this place. There was no address marker, no company title on a placard or illuminated marquee. Nada. We didn't need directions since we'd studied the map beforehand, but I realized there weren't any driving signs on the property either. That anonymity was too obvious.

Oh, I know who you are in there.

According to plan, Jonah drove the truck down the driveway, around to the southwest corner of the facility. That was the direct path to the double bay entrance where deliveries were brought and wastes were picked up.

With a slight jolt, the truck rocked at Jonah's braking and parking. I hadn't spotted a single employee on the property in the drive up, and as we sat there in the high cab, I surveyed the double bay garage space. As though this specific parking area was a cave, we were hidden down there with the truck. The truck's rear butted up to the raised platform where material could be carted into the cargo space. Concrete surrounded us on three sides, with the pavement sloping up.

Wastes were held in the basement, and the opening we'd driven through to get down here showed that the ground level was more like the first floor.

"I see four so far," Jonah said quietly.

"How old are you?" I scoffed. "You've got bad eyes already?" I'd counted seven surveillance cameras. Still, we'd expected them. Zero had shown detailed satellite images of the entire exterior. There should be a total of nine in this semi-underground parking space. Even though I'd been informed ahead of time that we'd be watched by their security team, I feared someone seeing me and making a connection to Cassidy, since they'd known we were together. Or, worse, that someone was watching the feed and would nitpick and notice we Dixon brothers weren't the waste disposal workers they usually saw.

Sitting in the truck's cab any longer would only make someone even more suspicious of our presence. So together, like planned, we exited the truck simultaneously and went to the closed garage door Jonah had backed up to.

I tapped in the passcode to the lock—numbers Zero had found by hacking the waste disposal's records and securing the specified sequence used for entrance.

With a soft hiss, the garage door opened. Creaks sounded as the slab was lifting on the chain.

I stood still, muscles bunched as if an attack would spring out at us. Nothing. I exhaled the breath I'd been holding and peered inside. Rolling laundry containers filled with white fabrics lined the wall to the right. To my left, there were HVAC units, tall blocks humming away. All I cared about was the absence of people who might immediately notice us. Jonah and I hadn't come up with much more of a plan to this phase of the breach except to pretend to collect the medical waste containers that would likely be labeled down here somewhere.

With no one watching us on this utility floor, there was no need to perfect our covers.

"Here we go," I mumbled to Jonah.

And so we began our rescue mission.

CHAPTER EIGHT
CASSIDY

Tami stared at me after finally telling me why she'd brought me here. Why she'd likely ordered her "recruits" to never kill me in the pursuit but to sedate me for transport here.

Me. Apparently the vessel to *her* DNA that she'd claimed possession to.

"You're not getting *anything* from me," I seethed.

I wasn't sure about having kids. I was too young. I had years to figure that out. Even with the full force of realizing and accepting my love for Luke, I hadn't dipped a toe in those particular waters. Did I love him? Hell yeah, I did. Did I want a future with him? Yes, however he could adjust to one with me. Did I want to have little Lukes and little Cassies running around? Maybe? I'd hardly had time to let this budding love stabilize while we'd been on the run.

My potential desire for a family aside, there was *no* way I'd want Tami to use me for any of her damn biogenetic goals.

"Says who?" she asked.

"Me." I knew she was taunting me to realize I was powerless here, but I wouldn't hesitate to stand up and at least vocally assert my will.

"Do you think that all the common patients who sacrificed their lives during our testing trials had any say?"

You evil, twisted piece of shit. "Sacrifices?" I spat.

She'd taken refuges, babies, criminals—all people who'd had no voice. She was nothing more than an organized mass murderer.

Ignoring me, she asked, “Do you think I’d have any problem holding you down and collecting what’s rightfully mine?”

“I’m not yours.”

“*I* will be the one to determine what belongs to *me*.” She leaned against the counter where the computer equipment sat. “Once that vial is delivered, we’ll prepare for the procedure.”

“Good luck.”

“I’ve never needed *luck*.”

“But you need that vial,” I said, my bravado increasing the more I thought about an inanimate item like the objective thing it was—unlike my very being.

“My security team will secure it.”

I shrugged. “Maybe, but the time’s running out. I’m no *genius* like you, but I bet the longer the vial is exposed to warmth, that DNA inside will start to unravel.”

She slammed her lips into a thin line. “And if that happens, we’ll have Scott’s code to identify the axolotls to get more of the beta DNA.”

I grinned, showing her my teeth. Stretching my lips so far reopened the cut from her slapping me and I let the blood drip. "Nope."

"You'll give us his code, just like Rosa gave us hers. She wasn't strong enough and caved quite quickly."

I soured at remembering Rosa's confession. That they tortured her, bluffed that they were killing me before her eyes and left her locked in a room with the corpse.

"Nope."

Tami cocked her head to the side. "I'll kill her."

"That'd actually be the *only* merciful thing you're capable of."

"You'd let her die?"

No. I swallowed hard. "She'd want it that way." The truth. I spoke it as my own bluff, but it wasn't a lie. Rosa told me not to risk saving her. It was the dangerous leverage I didn't want to consider.

"I'll bring her in here right now, then." She lowered her crossed arms and unhooked her ankles. Snapping from her cool posture, she held too much energy. "I'll wheel her in and get that part out of the way."

I tensed at her moving toward the door. "I won't give it to you." My voice only went shaky on the last word, but I couldn't stomach her leaving my sight. She'd as good as promised she'd kill Rosa. I had to keep her with me, away from my real mother.

"You can cut me up and take my eggs. I can't stop you. I'm not stupid. You can drug me up and I'll be defenseless."

"Of course."

"But you can't crack open my head and extract my mind."

"There are other ways to break one's mind."

Torture. How could I be related to this monster? Did even a shard of a conscience exist in her anymore? Or had her quest of immortality and a new form of humans destroy her completely?

I wasn't all that familiar with torture techniques, and I didn't want to discover the gory details about them.

Faced with such wicked intent, I zoned out, staring at Tami. I blanked out and thought of Luke. The cocooning comfort he offered in his arms. That soul-deep show of trust and compassion in every hold of his hands. *Please. Help me be strong.*

"I will not break. Not for you."

Tami's laugh grated at my nerves. "You won't defeat me in this." She came close, her flat heels smacking hard on the linoleum floor, her doctor outfit a costume over the stalking predator she was. Gripping my chin, she wrenched my face toward her. Between clenched teeth, she gritted out more promises. "I will take what I want."

"What good are my eggs when you don't have the beta DNA?"

She snarled. "I will take that however I need to. I'll scour the entire damn lake and take everything alive until I find what I need. I will—"

A bestial roar cut her off and her fingers dug into my flesh harder, like a reflexive reaction to being surprised.

The roar weaved into a scream and Tami released me. She stepped back from me, heading for the door. Elena. She'd woken in such a rage, she burst free of the bindings that had kept her down to her hospital bed.

"Ohmigod." It came out on a pant of air. I stared as she rose from the bed, no—launched from the reclined surface. Where she'd been out, silent and asleep, she was now shoving to her feet. One arm was thicker, fatter and swollen than the other, but as she hauled herself to stand, the limb receded to normal size again. She heaved an animalistic whine and grunted. Her face pulled on her features, thinning her lips as she bared her clenched teeth and her wrinkles creasing deep as she narrowed her eyes.

Dr. Jekyll and Mr. Hyde? Holy hell. I trembled, trapped and helpless with a monster in the making.

"Jolene!" Tami swore as she jabbed at a button on the door handle. "Unlock this now." She fumbled for a walkie-talkie device in her pocket and rushed to order, "I need you to unlock the door."

"But you said you wanted privacy—" The radio button clicked off.

Elena lunged at Tami. Her arms snaked around her chest, sending the walkie-talkie clattering to the floor. Wheezing hard, high-pitched breaths, Elena growled as she tackled the woman who wanted pieces of me. Together, they fell to the floor.

"Elena!"

Forget the horrific images of a demonic possession. Elena fought Tami without mercy, punching her and reaching to strangle her. She already *was* a demon. A she-Hulk.

"Elena!" I tried again.

As frightening as her one-eighty in strength and prowess was, at least she was firmly on my side now.

Strapped to my chair, I couldn't help her. She didn't flinch from my yells, unrelenting in her assault on Tami.

"You…you…goddamn…" Elena wailed a cry of pure agony. "Goddamn…*puta*!"

Tami's eyes glittered with anger as she stared up at Elena.

"You…play with…" Elena shook and strained, seemingly ripping from a hell inside out as she struggled to overcome her body's rapid changes. "You play with life and death. And now it's your turn to…suffer! You want to…" Another growl. "Talk about a last time? You'll get yours now!"

"I'm the boss here," Tami got out between pants. Then she bucked, trying to throw Elena off of her. No longer pinned between her latest patient, the women stood and fought for a chokehold.

Jesus. Christ! I tried to catch my breath, watching the violence and wishing I could help instead of sitting here like a pointless spectator. Confrontations weren't my thing, but dammit, I'd lost my passive nature sometime during my life on the run. However, it didn't matter how much I wriggled and squirmed, my arms and legs were not going to slide out of these straps.

"I will *end* you!" Elena bellowed. She reared back to kick her bare foot at Tami's head.

I blinked, stunned by the violence and…damn. I didn't think a person could be *that* flexible to deliver such a kick in that proximity. With the Last Time treatment, Elena had adopted some Bruce Lee-worthy moves. Or the fire within her body fueled her to such rage and strength.

Tami stumbled back and Elena dove on top of her. They landed just at my feet and I craned down to see, wishing I could crawl back and be further away from this fight. Both women stuck their arms out, trying to choke out the other.

Heaving hard breaths, Elena sounded like a wounded animal battling its adversary. Her curly black hair was sweaty and matted to her face where it wasn't flying about. A strand tickled against my calf.

"I will *end* you!" she repeated.

Tami trembled under Elena's grasp on her neck. Both of them were Xols, but I hoped that since Elena was on top, she might possess superior inhuman power with that Last Time dose they'd given her. She was unpredictably strong, but I feared she'd crash again, like she had not long ago.

She needed to take Tami *out*. Disable her for at least a moment—long enough for me to get the hell out of this chair so I could do something. Choking her didn't seem to be working, but what else could she do? All she had were her bare hands and unimaginable rage.

Tami's elbow flung out and knocked into the toe of my shoe. I curled my toes, trying to avoid any touch with her. But—

What the hell?

I wriggled my toes again, sliding the sole of my foot against the cushion of my shoe. Something hard was…

Oh my God! My foot was rubbing along the slim switchblade Tramer had given me in Mexico. It was so thin and short, I'd forgotten it was even there, snug in my shoe.

"Elena!"

Her reply was a grunt.

"Elena! In my shoe!"

My legs were tied to the chair but I could rotate my ankle a little. I jerked it side to side, trying to free my footwear. It got her attention, at least.

"Take it. In my shoe."

She made eye contact for one halting moment. Her pupils were dilated and huge. Bloodshot and crazed. Still, she looked to my feet. I kept wriggling.

On a loud growl, Elena headbutted Tami and kept her hand on her throat.

Tami wasn't knocked out, but she wasn't able to stop Elena from moving her other hand to my shoe. Her fingers shook with too much force, but she yanked off my shoe. The slim knife dropped to the floor and she grabbed it.

Tami groaned at the sight of the switchblade flicking open in Elena's hand. "Don't—"

Elena roared as she slammed the knife to Tami's heart.

I winced at the blood staining the white lab coat. I looked away for a moment, the only sounds in the room Elena's harsh, heaving wheezes and my rushed pants for air. I swallowed hard and looked back down, avoiding the knife wound entirely.

"It won't…stop her." Elena eased off of Tami, who'd dropped her arms.

"Not for long." I didn't know what timeframe could be expected for her to regenerate, but I wasn't going to waste a second of it.

"Need to end her," Elena said, reaching toward Tami. She swiped the switchblade on her filthy jungle outfit and then pushed to stand. Her whole body shuddered as she stood and walked to me, like she was still experiencing the aftershocks of an electrocution. She slid the knife under my forearm, her shaking so bad she sliced my skin. "I…" Squeezing her eyes shut tight, she took a deep breath. "I won't last…"

With her one swift move, the knife was thrust up and cut through the strap. The first strap was free.

She released the knife and dropped to the floor, convulsing even more. "End her…Cassidy. End her…"

I craned to retrieve the knife, pulling even harder in the stretch. Stings spread on my wrist until I thought I'd crack something, but finally, I fingered the hilt of the knife. Straining more, I watched Elena as she flopped in a seizure on the ground.

One more push and…there. I felt the warm handle between my fingertips. Got it!

I sat up, dizzy from leaning so low at such an awkward angle, and swiped the knife at my bindings. Nothing. Jesus. It was the same knife. Elena had just barely moved her hand. She possessed *that* much energy and force as she'd been weakening. Sawing back and forth, I made slow progress at the strap. Every other motion back and forth, I checked that Tami was lying still on the floor and Elena was still breathing, albeit trembling.

"Hang on, Elena." I got my other arm free. I whooshed out a breath of relief and hunched down to start on my legs. "Just hang on."

She'd stopped jerking as chaotically, shivering now. "I…I don't want to. This is no way…to live…"

No way to live. Her honesty tugged at my heartstrings and I pitied her fate. She was right. Being given the Last Time was nothing but a cruel yo-yo on the edge of life and death. With both my hands on the knife, I was able to double up on my efforts. I nearly had my leg free. "Thank you," I told her.

She wheezed hard breaths and I watched as she closed her eyes. "Use…the gun."

A gunshot wound wouldn't stop a Xol for good. I knew *some* Xols could be ended. Vinh had died in the plane to Mexico, but there was no way to know how different of a mutant he was to Tami. Killing these freaks was something I hadn't tested much yet.

"The drug…gun…" she said.

"The tranquilizer?"

Her head bobbed slightly. "B—blue."

Blue tranq gun. Got it.

"Used it…on me. When I woke up deranged… like this. It can…take them out for a bit."

All right. The blue tranq gun wasn't Xol-proof. It was first on my list.

I finally freed myself and stood fully, rubbing at my wrists. Blood smeared a sticky trail down to my elbow from the cut Elena had accidentally given me with her unsteady hands. I lowered to the floor and gripped her shoulder.

“Find the blue gun. Don’t…take chances she won’t wake up.”

I stood, understanding there wasn’t anything I could do for her. Anger sparked anew as I considered her fate. She was dying and then was rushed back to life. Now she’d linger in pain and rage without the chance for peace. There would be no end to her torment as her body would continuously refuse to surrender, regenerating at any injury.

“Get…Rosa…” she whispered. “And get out of here.”

Then she went slack.

CHAPTER NINE

LUKE

No one was downstairs on the utility floor.

We walked into the building, carefully following hallways we'd studied earlier. If we hadn't so thoroughly quizzed each other on the route, we would've been beyond lost. So many turns and forked hallways. From the exterior, the building didn't seem too complex. Inside, though, everything was a much larger maze.

While it was a help that no employees ambled on the basement floor, and there were no chances of someone asking what the contracted waste disposal people were doing away from the waste containers near the truck we'd parked, it was just as much a problem. We couldn't get upstairs in these uniforms, which meant we needed to encounter at least a couple of staff members.

Stealing—well, borrowing—others' garments wasn't something I enjoyed, but it had worked in duping the cartel and it'd been a success so far as Jonah and I posed as the waste pickup workers. We were going to stick with what worked.

"Where is everyone?" Jonah asked in a whisper as we passed by what looked like a kitchen area.

I shrugged. It was nighttime. I imagined the only people who'd come down to this floor were maintenance and auxiliary staff and they weren't the sort to have projects this late.

We couldn't go upstairs until we had disguises to let us blend in with the Xol team here. The hiccup of searching for someone to get the outfits from irked me more than it should. Already, I was losing my focus and alert edge. For every step I took in the underbelly of this mad science show's site, I couldn't shake the urgency to get to Cassidy. She was here, somewhere—so far, yet so close, it messed with my mind.

Jonah paused at a corner of the hallway, halting me from walking to the right. With his finger to his lips, I listened for what could have alerted him.

Faint voices, their tones too low to be understood. A man and a woman? Maybe it was two men? I nodded at my brother to acknowledge his discovery.

Without a sound, I removed the slim mask from my back pocket. It was a replica of the one Dale had brought with him to spring us from the police station in Oklahoma. Jonah removed one from his back pocket too, giving me a dubious side-eye. I understood his hesitation. As far as face protection went, these were very flexible and slim. By appearances only, it would seem they were too flimsy and cheap. I nodded again, encouraging him to put his on, and strapped mine to my face. Then I reached into my front pocket for one of the small gas discs that would knock people down.

Jonah pulled the first strap over his head and let the device hang below his neck, still reluctant to put the top strap on as well. "Will that really work on people?" He pointed at the small, circular item in my hand.

I nodded and then winced. Yes and no. All the police officers and personnel in the police station had dropped like flies. When my mask slipped off, I'd dozed instantly. Jolene, though, she hadn't been affected at all. Then again, she was impervious to sedative gas *and* fire, so that made her less of a person and more of a mutant.

"If they're human, yes," I reiterated. Dale and I had gone over this step earlier.

"Everyone's human."

I shook my head. "Xols are something more."

"So if they drop, they're like us. If they aren't bothered, they're superfreaks."

I nodded again. We were hoping for the former. Normal humans would be easiest to knock out and tie up—they'd be on par with our strengths. If those voices we'd overheard belonged to Xol mutants, we didn't have a true way to keep them down.

That tranq did drop Michael, though... I couldn't figure it out, how a simple sedative would have knocked down that beast of a monster. It must have been something different to work fast, even on Xol bodies, but it wasn't lasting since he'd be gone by the time I'd returned to the refuge.

Blinking quickly with his brows raised, Jonah sighed. He slid his mask on and met my gaze. I doubted he was convinced, but he was ready to face our risk. Besides, seeing was believing and all that.

I turned the corner of the hallway and led my brother closer to the source of the quiet conversation. A doorway was wide open, and at the start of a window, I stopped. Inside were a couple of tables with chairs, a long countertop with a sink, drying mat holding upside-down coffee mugs, coffeemaker, and other lunchroom odds and ends.

A staff breakroom? It seemed like it. I pressed the tab to the disc in my hand and launched it toward the open doorway. The circle spun like a top and a chair was pushed back.

"What the—"

A thud followed a moment after the man had tried to ask his question.

I gave it thirty more seconds before I approached the room.

Two men had been enjoying coffees and donuts. One mug had splashed out the black liquid when the taller guy's head dropped to the table. On the floor lay the other lab-coated man. One of them snored lightly and we rushed to get to work.

They were wearing khakis—like Jonah and I were—so we only took their button-down shirts and lab coats. Couldn't forget their nametags and keycards attached to retractable lanyards. Disguising ourselves as human Xol workers didn't take long, but once we stood and adjusted the clothing, I realized Jonah had the same issue as me.

The shirts were like a second skin, the buttons damn-near ready to burst off.

"Ready when you are," Jonah said, wincing as he tried to tug his shirt sleeves down beneath the lab coat.

"Up we go."

Dressed as the Xol staff, we didn't walk quite as slowly as we had as the waste disposal guys. Side by side, we worked off memory and headed toward the elevators. It was still empty in the basement, and it was a brief relief that we'd trespassed this far without a snafu.

Don't think too far. Don't...jinx it, dammit.

Inside the elevator, Jonah used his stolen key fob to activate the car. He pressed the button for the third floor, where the blueprint had shown most of what seemed to be medical exam rooms. As we lifted, my stomach dropped, which didn't help my rising anxiety.

We're here. We'll find her and bolt. Not long now. I inhaled a deep breath.

"We got this, man," Jonah whispered, like he was too nervous to speak louder when it was just the two of us in here. Safe in the air of the car and well beyond the reach of the gas bomb I'd activated, we removed our masks and shoved them into our lab coat pockets.

"Yeah." I couldn't speak more than that past the lump in my throat. As much as it tugged on my conscience for asking Jonah to put himself in harm's way for me—for Cassidy—I was damned grateful he was there. Encouraging me, reassuring me he had my back. Jonah wasn't a weak wuss or an ignorant fighter. He was brave, didn't take shit, and happened to excel in martial arts.

"Thanks," I said to break the silence in what felt like the longest damn elevator ride ever.

He raised his brows in question.

"For being here. Helping me."

He huffed. "I'm still shocked you even asked me."

I allowed a nervous smile. "Maybe I finally realized you might not be a little boy anymore."

Rolling his eyes, he opened his mouth to speak. The elevator stopping and buoying in the suspension of the brakes cut him off. The doors swooshed open, presenting us a view of people working in what looked like a hospital floor. A wide hallway ran both ways, rooms sectioned off in equal, symmetrical intervals. Glass walls and door provided glimpses inside, showing hospital beds with men and women lying down. The thick shackles trapping many of them to the beds didn't hint at much willingness.

Xol patients? They had to be.

I ground my teeth, squashing the fear that Cassidy would now be one of them. That she was no longer a mere human like me, but the beginning of a monster who wouldn't be able to control her life or body. Stepping out of the elevator with Jonah, I roved my stare along the rooms that didn't have curtains concealing the occupants.

She could be hooked up to an IV, pumped up with God knows what—

"I don't care. Get the motherfucking vial one way or another."

I braced an arm over Jonah's chest as soon as I heard that voice.

Michael.

Hell, no…

He'd been walking to the elevator, talking on a cell phone. As I hadn't moved out of the way of the elevator's entrance, stunned at the amount of rooms housing Xol patients, he'd nearly plowed right into us.

His eyes narrowed just before he ran toward us.

Hell, yes, that's the son of a bitch again. No doubt about it. My recurring nightmare really was right there, barreling into me.

Jonah grunted as one of the two minions who'd been walking with Michael slammed him back into the elevator. Advantaged enough to see the bull of a man charging at me, I braced for the impact. He crashed into me, sending both of us into the elevator.

I was no stranger to his tactics and strength. Fierce power and a preference to cut off my air.

Still, I groaned at the full-bodied shove into the elevator's wall. Four men, none of them small, fought in the confined square of the elevator. Jonah and I wrestled with our attackers, and in a blur of a glance with my peripheral vision, I saw the remaining man enter the elevator and press the button for the doors to close.

I didn't care where they were taking me, and I was certain we'd caught Michael by surprise, if the initial expression of his frown was any indicator. Wherever they wanted to take this fight was fine by me. Because it was going to be our last one. Pummeling my fists into his face and side, I threw all my rage into my assault. Defense. It was impossible to know who was winning at the moment. I was alive, so that meant we had to be somewhat evenly matched for now.

The elevator dipped again. The distraction of the motion must have been the trick Jonah needed, because in the small space of the car, he jump-kicked the Xol freak and sent him crashing into the opposite wall.

"Go back down there," Jonah said as the second minion lunged for him.

Michael held me in a headlock, so similar to how he'd tried to strangle me the very first time we met. The first minion shook his head and began to stand, so I pushed into Michael's hold to jump up and kick both feet at the man's chest. He went sprawling back again, I gasped for air, and Jonah continued to beat the other guy to no avail.

"You're a pain in the ass, you know that?" Michael gritted out. "All we want to do is advance the human race and you can't stop interfering."

We? He had that much say in Xol missions? He was the Project's very first patient to be called a success, but what else did he do here? Obviously, he was in security or law enforcement for the team to have come after Cassidy and the data, but his comment seemed to intimate.

Jonah roared, the sound echoing loud in the tight space, nearly drowning out the deafening drum of my pulse in my ears. He spun and kicked at both of the minions, smacking one into Michael. It was just enough of a shift to the wall that I could twist my face to the side. I gasped in a breath and threw my head back to his.

Shit. Stars danced in my eyes at the hard hit, but his arm dropped from my neck. Before I could even stand up straight and cease the dizziness of too little oxygen, I attacked him. It felt like an hour, but eventually, I had him pinned to the floor. Blood was splattered everywhere—his or mine, likely both.

"What the hell do you want from us?" I seethed as he struggled to wrench my fingers away from his neck. "Why did you take Cassidy?"

Down on the ground next to us was Jonah and one of the Xol men. The second guy was unconscious in a heap in the corner of the elevator. Jonah still fought hard, wrestling into a roll out of the elevator. I had to trust that he'd finish that freak. I couldn't help him. I had to get answers to find Cassidy.

"Tami needed her. To begin the reproduction of the next generation of Xol recruits." He grinned at me despite the redness of his face proving he wasn't having fun without proper air to his lungs. His eyes watered yet he still smiled. "And I've never failed to deliver for my woman."

His woman? He and Tami were together beyond the workplace? I scoffed, not calm enough to find amusement at this. What, he fell in love with her for giving him the first dose of human-tested Xol cure? And she'd kept him along as her guinea pig-turned-lover?

How…pathetic.

"Cassidy isn't yours to use for anything," I vowed. She was *mine*. She belonged *with* me and not to be manipulated by anything or anyone, least of all these people.

"Too late," he sneered as his lips began to turn blue.

The hell it was too late. I was here, and I wasn't leaving without her. "Where is she?" I demanded, choking him harder.

He shifted his arm and I heard a click. "Code four," he said.

Without removing my hands from his neck, I glanced to the side.

In his hand was a walkie-talkie he must have had in his pocket or on his belt.

"Code four. Lockdown *now*."

The elevator door slid open and beyond was the hallway to the third floor again.

"Where is she?" I demanded again.

He didn't answer, his eyes rolling back. My fingers ached from the tension of gripping him so hard and I loosened them a fraction. Just as I removed one hand from him, alarms blared in the background.

We were locked in—simple humans against monsters.

And I still needed to find Cassidy.

Shit.

CHAPTER TEN

CASSIDY

Blue tranq gun.

Blue tranq gun.

Blue tranq gun.

I wanted whatever defense I could have before I got to Rosa. If I set foot outside this room, Jolene would probably be there, waiting for her master's orders. I wouldn't survive a second past her once she realized Tami lay on the floor, unconscious, yet somehow breathing.

Scrambling away from Elena, I slipped on the blood on the floor. I gasped, fearing the noise of me smashing into the rollaway stool would wake up Tami. With a quick glance, I checked that she was out.

On my hands and knees, I crawled toward her. Bile rose fast in my throat.

So much…blood.

I swallowed hard, willing myself not to faint. As I gingerly felt around in Tami's lab coat pockets, I watched her head—to avoid looking at the wound on her chest and to be somewhat ready if she were to suddenly jerk upright like a wound-up deranged clown in a jack-in-the-box.

Nothing was in there. No blue tranq gun. I scooted away from her and my hand brushed against something hard.

The walkie-talkie. Its back case had fallen loose, and I jammed it together. Having communication outside the room could be a help, but no one out there would listen to *me*, the captive *thing* with coveted ova.

It was still such a twisted thought, that this diabolical and insane woman sought me out to take my *eggs*. I ignored the return of disbelief and rushed to the counter. Cabinets hung on the wall above the computer monitor, but there were no blue tranq guns in there. I couldn't find any drugs or weapons at all. Neither was there anything of help in the three drawers below the countertop's surface.

I returned to the door and jimmied the handle. It didn't give. I debated pounding on the panel and pretending to be Tami. Jolene could open the door, I could hide behind it as it swung in, and then I could pull her into the space and squeeze out past her, locking *her* in with Tami and Elena.

No, not really. It wouldn't work. For one, she was faster and stronger than me. And—

Radio static came on the walkie-talkie. "Code four."

Code four? I frowned and peered at the device. My heart pumped faster, panic setting in. Code? A code of any kind in a medical environment had to mean something horrible.

"Code four. Lockdown *now*," the masculine voice said.

"Lockdown?" I mumbled to myself. "Yeah, that'll fucking help!" I was already locked in a room with a woman undergoing some extreme Xol metamorphosis and a certifiable killer. I didn't need to be trapped in this place even more.

Alarms began to wail and I cringed. Crap. This was bad. This was worst than the baddest bad. I tuned out the *wee-wah* looping over and over and ignored the bright red light flickering above the door. The door that began to open.

I stepped back as the door pushed into the room an inch.

"Dr. Shaw?" Jolene asked, her high heel clacking once as she set one foot inside. Up higher, the end of metal cylinder poked in, a gun barrel. Another move forward, as though she felt the need to enter with a weapon leading the way, and I saw that it wasn't a handgun with bullets, but a device to administer a dart.

Blue!

"Lockdown's commenced and—"

I slammed forward and shoved the door shut on her arm and foot. Surprise was all I'd had in the impromptu move, but it worked. The tranq gun dropped to the floor but she shoved against the wood, forcing me back. I began to fall, but I rolled into the drop, dodging to the side, and snatched the tranq gun.

My hands shook, but I didn't choke this time. I pulled the trigger, aiming at her arm against the door. With this close of a range, I really didn't have a chance of missing.

She screamed, the sound fading to a crooked mewl as she dropped.

Panting and stunned that it had actually worked, I pushed to stand. The gun still had two more darts in a strange-looking adapter.

Stepping over Jolene in the doorway, I glanced back at Elena still asleep on the floor. Then I checked Tami. Still out as well.

But she won't stay down. I almost shot another dart into her to buy myself more time, but I couldn't. Who knew what would hold me back from getting to

Rosa? I might need to sedate whoever stood between me and my real mother.

I kept the tranq gun in front of me and exited into the hallway. Workers—nurses and lab techs, by the way of their clothes—went from room to room along the hall, a more frantic bustle of activity than there had been before this lockdown had been declared. At the very end of the hallway, an elevator waited with its doors wide open.

I squinted at the shape of a man on the ground. One, no, two people were on the ground. The man who was lying on the floor had his leg out far enough to stop the opened elevator doors from shutting. On top of him—

"Luke!"

He turned at my voice. I ran to him, desperate to be with him and make sure this wasn't a cruel hallucination. Closer and closer, I ran, near enough to watch as Michael sat up and punched Luke off of him.

I skidded to a stop, my shoes rubbing the soles onto the smooth surface of the floor. Wind-milling my arms, I retreated in a scramble for cover.

Luke dropped to the floor as Michael stood, cracking his neck.

Dammit! He began to leave the elevator, his stare locked on mine.

I refused to turn my back to him, watching as he scowled at me, and dashed back into the room.

Shit. Shit. Shit. Shit. I eyed the room. It was just as I'd left it, only now I was a thousand times more scared and out of options. Michael was coming for me. I had two tranq darts but I was a lousy shot. If I aimed at him from too far away, I'd miss. It seemed my shooting precision *was* beginner's luck—only successfully hitting Michael in the library in Texas. If I waited for him to get closer, he'd be in the ideal range to shoot something at *me*.

My hands trembled as I paced in the exam room, careful not to step in the blood.

I didn't have time. Michael was coming for me, likely stomping his way down the thirty-some yards to me.

Close the door. I backed up to it but didn't shut it. If I dragged Jolene in here and shut it, I'd be locked again. And Michael would be out there to access Rosa—wherever she'd been taken.

Shoot him. I shook my head, knowing it was a fat chance of success.

I looked at Elena, still on the floor.

Tami. I checked to make sure she was still out.

Tami.

If Michael was coming, he'd need to see the tables had turned.

I ran to the drawers beneath the counters and removed an IV needle. My fingers shook as I ripped the package off. It wasn't as big as a syringe, and close enough, anyone could see it was an empty bluff. From a distance, though, it had to resemble a shot.

Without thinking about the gore of it, I lowered to Tami on the floor. I held my breath as I slid my hands under her shoulders. There was no way I could stomach looking at her blood, and as I eased my forearms past her armpits, I gagged. Warm stickiness coated me as I hauled her up by the armpits. Hugging her to me, I dragged her out of the room.

Seemed I was late to my high-noon duel in the hallway.

Michael stood there, a *real* gun at the ready, hanging in his hand at his hip. At his feet lay Luke. He rolled over, groaning but not getting up or even opening his eyes.

Seeing the man I loved so wounded *again*, I fought the urge to lash out.

This was enough. And I swore, to Hendrick, to Elena, to Rosa—I *would* end this.

"What happened to her?" Michael demanded, raising the gun to me.

I smirked. "Oh. Like you'd really kill me? I know what you want and it doesn't involve me being dead."

His eyes were steely and icy as he stared me down. "*We* control life and death here." He shrugged one shoulder. "I can shoot you and give you the Last Time and *still* take what rightfully belongs to Tami."

I shook my head, sick of hearing how these people thought they owned me. That they could hold power over anyone they pleased.

"The Last Time?" I asked, cocking my head to the side. "You mean this?" I shifted Tami's deadweight in my arm and jabbed the IV insert to her neck, threatening to pierce her skin with what I hoped he'd believe was a syringe of their latest development.

"Don't." Michael held his hand up, keeping the gun steady at me. "It's too much for her."

"But we had such an interesting chat. She's all about having the power."

"It will overwhelm her. She can't have more of the cure."

I shrugged.

In my next breath, I regretted my idea. All one hundred percent of my rash scheme.

Michael redirected his gun to Luke. "I'll kill him."

Life and death. They truly did play with both. If Michael shot Luke, I knew he wouldn't want the agony of being forced back to the living, the pain of going insane at the too-rapid transformation into a Xol. Not that anyone working here would want Luke to survive.

I bit my lip and forced my knees not to buckle.

I spiraled fast into heartache at the threat of losing Luke, *my* Luke, the strong yet gentle love that I'd never find in anyone else again. I shook my head and fumbled to keep Tami upright.

He couldn't.

He can't.

Luke is supposed to stay with me. I chose him. I chose us.

"You don't want to do this, Cassidy." Michael shook his head. "You can't. She's your mother. You can't hurt your *mother*."

A hand pushed into my shoulder blade and I gasped at the touch, at the shock that someone had crept up behind me. So stunned, I fell forward with Tami.

"The hell with that." Rosa snarled at Michael. "*I'm* her mother."

She didn't give him a chance to argue semantics. Over my shoulder, she fired a blue tranq dart straight at Michael's chest.

CHAPTER ELEVEN

LUKE

I clamped my teeth together at the sharp stab in my leg.

It had to be right there. In the same damn side I'd been shot before, in the same damn area of the bullet wound I was *still* recovering from.

As soon as I heard Rosa's voice, I'd snapped to. It had to have been a dream. Michael had really knocked me into another galaxy.

I could have sworn I'd heard Cassidy calling my name. I saw her. Or maybe my desperation to be with her again was messing with my mind.

Rosa…I'd heard her clearly though. She was mad—no, pissed off.

And now I was shot in the damn leg again. Lying on my side, I curled into a ball and pressed my hand to the wound. I opened my eyes, squinting against the brightness of red. On, off. On, off. It flashed like an angry finger shaking at me, scolding me for something bad.

There wasn't a light in the elevator though.

As the grogginess faded, a persistent wail broke through the haze.

Michael had called for a lockdown. Then, I'd thought I'd heard Cassidy.

"Luke!"

There it was again, her sweet voice cutting through the cry of the alarm. What in the hell was going on? I opened my eyes wider, blinking hard. I wasn't in the elevator anymore. In the middle of the hallway, nurses scrambled away from me, the few remaining workers who nearby stayed back from me and Michael. He lay next to me, unmoving in a massive heap of lethal killing power.

"Luke!"

No. I definitely heard her. Hadn't I?

Cassidy?

I craned my neck to find her. Her face was clear, if bloody, and there was no sign she was injured. Her mouth gaped at me, like she couldn't believe she was seeing *me*. Such pure love and relief in those bright blue eyes. Panting, she rolled an unconscious woman off her lap, got to her feet, and ran.

Shit. It *was* her!

Her footsteps pattered on the floor, tiny vibrations I felt with my cheek pressed to the cold surface. "Luke!"

Every step she took closer to me spiked me with elation.

She was alive.

Right here.

This gorgeous woman I couldn't live without.

She was *alive* and coming back to me.

"Luke?" Rosa asked.

Before my girl could crash into me, I caught a glimpse of my neighbor standing just behind where

Cassidy had been sitting with that lifeless woman. Rosa remained where she was as she watched my reunion with Cassidy, pressing one hand to her stomach, the other clutching the same kind of tranq gun I'd used on Michael in Mexico.

Cassidy dove to her knees to cradle me to her. One deep breath of her, and I was home. Her hands and arms trembled as she held me to her, squeezing tight. Already, my pain ebbed and my fears faded. In her arms, I'd always be at peace. I struggled to trust this perfect moment. Wanting to be with her and *knowing* she was okay had consumed me since the moment she ran away from the fight in Xochimilco.

She's alive. Right here. I was so swarmed with love and relief, I was stupefied to move past that mantra.

She's alive and right here with me.

"Goddammit, Cassie," I said into her neck, trapping her down to me with one arm. I couldn't sit up yet. Not until I compressed my wound. Keeping her close wasn't enough, and I clung to her. "I was so scared."

She huffed, the sassy sound ruined with a sob. "You, scared?"

Her feistiness soothed me, promising me she was still the same. Still the Cassidy I loved with every miserable bit of my soul.

I pressed my lips to her warm skin, her neck, her chin, anywhere I could nestle close enough in our awkward hold.

Another slight hiss sounded and we parted to look back.

Rosa was still there, the tranq gun aimed at the woman on the floor. A small blue dart was embedded in her neck. "They won't stay down for long."

Cassidy gingerly released me but didn't let go. Instead, she moved both to help me sit up and inspect my leg. "He shot you."

I winced at the pain lancing through my leg at the adjustment. Grin and bear it. This wasn't enough to keep me down and defenseless, dammit. I kept the leg positioned straight out and gripped my thigh above the wound site.

At the cautious urgency to her voice, I knew I'd have to truly rejoice "rescuing" Cassidy later. We were still locked in the Xol facility. Workers—nurses, and lab helpers—milled in the hallway not far from us. I hadn't come this far to find Cassidy only to not get us the hell away from here. We were nowhere near in the clear yet.

"Get away from him," Rosa called firmly over the din of the alarm. "There's no telling when he'll get up after the sedative."

I tried to roll onto my hands and knees, Cassidy's small, warm body holding me up at my side. "I'd say you bought us maybe ten minutes, tops." If I'd shot Michael with the same thing Rosa just had, I knew he'd fallen down but escaped in that short of a reprieve.

Jonah joined Rosa in the hallway, limping in his step. In his arms, he held several devices. "Well, I found more," he told the elderly woman.

Rosa nodded at him and took another tranq gun from my brother.

He'd slipped out of the elevator. I couldn't believe I'd lost track of that detail. Michael had been so close to ending my life, and as I'd neared passing out, I'd grown even more confused at Cassidy calling me.

He jogged lopsidedly to me and Cassidy. First, he gave us both a tranq gun, leaving the last one for himself. Then he ducked under my arm to help us hobble away.

Every step seemed to drain the life from me, and as we moved, I scoped the hallway. We were in a medical facility. There had to be some gauze and bandages somewhere in one of these rooms.

"Sorry I left you," he said between pants. "If I was going to be the last one standing, I had to take that chance to find her for you," he said.

That he'd escaped didn't faze me. He was an able-bodied man. He hadn't stuck around to save me in the elevator—not because he didn't have my back, but because he'd likely known he had to finish finding Cassidy for me. I squeezed his shoulder as he helped drag me toward Rosa. He'd get all my gratitude later.

"Jonah?" Cassidy asked.

"Oh." Jonah snorted a laugh. "Yeah, that's me."

"Where is he hit?" Rosa asked without looking at us as we grouped with her.

"In the leg." Her question was clinical, not something she'd wanted to know in some form of a bedside manner. She had yet to cease surveying the hallway, as though she was calculating the dangers and strategizing a way out. The fact I couldn't walk on my own was telling enough.

We needed to leave this place before the top leaders of Project Xol woke up. They weren't easy to kill, not with our means and levels of basic human strength. Being stuck in here—with me slowing everyone down even more—wasn't an ideal situation.

Jonah released me, letting me lean on my good leg, holding Cassidy. She stood strong beneath my added weight, her small fingers clutching the shirt at my side.

“I’ll handle it.” I gripped my tranq gun tighter, reminding myself I might be slower but I wasn’t down yet. “Good to see you,” I quipped.

She deadpanned at me. “Yes, but not like this.”

“Are you okay?” Cassidy asked Rosa.

“Until it’s me on the floor instead of them, I’ll make do.”

“But the poison…” Cassie said.

Rosa shook her head. “It’s no longer in me. I’m not…one hundred percent, but I’m okay. Once the alarms started, he”—she pointed in the direction where Jonah had gone—“came into my room and removed the IV. As soon as the line was severed, it was easier to breathe. He said he was looking for you and—” She flapped her arm out to the side. “We found you, all right.”

My brother hadn’t gone far, just into the nearest room. He returned almost immediately with white coils in his hand. Cassidy sighed at the sight of him. “You hold him up. I’ll…”

If it was possible, I loved her even more. She was willing to battle her phobia of blood for my sake.

"I can't hold him up as well as you can," she confessed.

Guilt knifed me, that I was causing her trouble or pain.

"Quickly," Rosa warned. "Others will come soon."

And we only had maybe a dozen shots of the only thing that could temporarily stop the mutants everywhere in this building.

Not even a beat later, as though Rosa's prediction summoned it, someone *did* approach us. "This floor is under lockdown—" a guard said as he ran up to us. His uniform labeled him as a security guard, but he lacked the unnatural muscular build of Xols.

I didn't hesitate. Cassidy lowered to the ground and began wrapping gauze around my thigh. Before I could wonder if this security guard was human or not, I raised the handgun still—somehow—tucked into my waistband at the small of my back and fired once at him.

He cried out, dropping down on the leg I hadn't shot in the knee.

Cassidy wrenched the gauze tighter and I winced.

"Is there any way to take these fuckers out?" Jonah asked as a trio of men came running from the other end of the hall. Tall, beefed-up, and scowling at us without any welcome, I anticipated these were Xol mutants. We'd lucked out with the first one showing up being human, but now we were seriously screwed.

"What's going on?" a woman screamed from one of the patient rooms.

Jolene? I narrowed my eyes at the blonde.

"What happened to Dr. Shaw?" she cried out hysterically.

"Oh, for God's sake. Not you again," Cassidy groaned. Finished with my leg, now securely tied maybe too tight—I wasn't going to nitpick her first-aid skills—she stood.

Jolene charged toward the woman with the bloodstained lab coat. "Dr. Shaw!"

Shaw?

"Just *shut up*," Cassidy snapped as she shot Jolene with the tranq gun. She missed, and Jonah fired one next, sticking a dart in her chest. She howled and then crumpled.

"Still learning how to aim?" he teased.

"Not *now*," I told him. We had to stick together and focus. He could save his jokes for later.

"Dr. Shaw?" I asked.

Rosa huffed. "More coming from ahead."

Cassidy glanced at the incoming Xol patients—some looking angry and confused as they left their rooms and others sprinting down the hallway as they entered from wherever else they'd been in the building. They were going to swarm as word got out that their leaders were unconscious on the floor.

Cassidy nodded. "That's Tami." Her sharp, curt way of introducing me to the woman who'd given birth to her was cold. I didn't assume it was some mommy-daughter turmoil she was evading, but the panic of having to face more tenacious enemies.

"What the hell are we going to do?" she asked.

We collected into a circular shape. Our backs weren't exposed as the four of us stood shoulder to shoulder. All of us had our hands raised with blue tranq guns pointed out in the direction of incoming attackers. Jonah and I doubled up and had a handgun in our nondominant hands as well.

This had to be it. We were outnumbered and outpowered—the goddamn theme of my life since I'd known about this secret science. Our Xol-effective darts wouldn't last us more than a minute.

We'd come so far and had fallen so short. It wouldn't take them long to regenerate past their injuries, and by then, we'd been more pawns to torture. Michael would get back up and gloat about always being able to pander to his woman.

Hope lingered in the recesses of my mind. A firm flash of determination remained—that where Jonah, Cassidy, Rosa, and I might fail at causing a setback inside this facility, Dale and Zero might be able to dismantle the organization from the outside.

I wasn't going to cede defeat. As long as I was breathing, I'd protect the woman I loved, fight for the good of humanity. There was no way to dismiss the pending surrender speeding toward us, but as we held each other up, not backing down, a calm washed over me.

"We'll follow this to the end," Rosa answered Cassidy.

We damn well will.

The only silver lining was the fact I'd been granted one last chance to kiss her again. To have another moment of peace in her arms.

We'll go down fighting.

CHAPTER TWELVE
CASSIDY

To the end.

It was here.

The end was right here in my face.

I wasn't being dramatic like Tami liked to accuse.

It was a bold-faced fact.

We had no ammo or physical stamina to withstand all these people heading toward us. Xol patients staggered out of their rooms, nurses in scrubs frowned at us as they stalked closer. Lab coats swished as tech and maybe other "doctors" approached.

Like a punk who'd poked a hole in a hive, these members of the Xol cult swelled up and swarmed to beat down the trespasser.

"I..." I gritted my teeth, loathing this feeling of helplessness. I'd overcome so many damn episodes of hell only to lose after all? It was... This was bullshit!

"I love you." I spoke the words before I wouldn't have the chance.

Luke deserved to know.

"No," he said. "Not now. You're going to tell me that when we're not stuck here like this."

I admired his spirit, his take-no-shit dominance. His rugged strength and unflinching drive to stand up to true killers bolstered my faith in survival, but...

There was no way we'd get past this many mutated people, all of them unhappy we'd disturbed the purpose of this place.

Like a flood, they rushed toward us. My fingers trembled but I refused to lower my tranq gun. A wave of their voices clashed louder and louder as they shortened the distance between us.

Oh my God.

Oh my God.

Oh my God.

I was wrong. I *still* sucked with confrontations. This wasn't a scrimmage, this was sitting vulnerable in the battlefield of a crusade.

Despite the air conditioning chilling the building, sweat collected and teased at my temple. I fidgeted, too attuned to the annoying sensation to ignore it. Rolling my shoulder, I tried to wipe at my face with my shirt sleeve, and in that motion, I froze.

Looking downward for just that brief moment, instead of staring at the angry-faced growing mob coming our way, I tracked a simple motion.

Something rolling.

Spinning.

Toppling into an oblong oval wobble.

A little circular plate. Just like—

"Luke!" I gripped his arm and dragged him to see.

He grunted as he shifted. Perhaps I'd jostled him too much in his wounded stance. Regardless of any discomfort I might have caused him, he heeded my call and he looked down just as the flat gas bomb began to emit a translucent azure cloud.

Blue? We'd deployed several of those sedative trinkets Dale had given us, but they'd all released toxins invisible to the eye.

Another puff of blue rose, snagging my attention toward where Michael still lay.

And one more, further down the hallway where Xol patients headed toward us.

And another. And another.

All along the seemingly never-ending hallway, more discs rolled and disengaged.

"Our masks!" Jonah said, reaching for his back pocket.

"What is this?" Rosa asked.

Luke shot out his arm, halting his brother from grabbing anything. "No. Look."

We did. Instead of staring at the azure haze spreading quickly through the air, rushing faster near HVAC vents, I gasped.

Xol mutants. The patients, the ones dressed normally like Jolene and Michael and Tami…

All of them were falling to the ground like hypnotized monsters.

We were still standing.

How in the hell…

I opened and closed my mouth, struggling to make sense.

"Now *that* works a helluva lot easier on them than shoving them outta my plane."

The man who spoke had called out his drawling greeting from down the hall.

I'd recognize that red hair anywhere.

"Fox?" I spluttered, still not lowering my tranq gun despite the Xol falling to the ground. The pilot who'd flown us to Mexico—Tramer's buddy.

"Hey!" he called out jubilantly, like this was an everyday occurrence.

As he came closer, others similarly dressed to him came forth. They'd dressed for stealth and defense, black cargo pants held up by a duty belt with all kinds of necessities for violence—cuffs, canisters, knives, guns, and ammo. Beneath their Kevlar vests, they wore black shirts, revealing their toned physique to kick ass.

Three of them, however, wore masks.

If they were protecting their faces, were they untrusting of the gas and paranoid, or…protecting themselves from breathing it in. Meaning—

I jerked my tranq gun toward the trio of tall soldiers not breathing in the blue air.

They were Xols? On…our side?

"Whoa, whoa, whoa…"

I turned toward the other deep voice, this one coming from the other end of the hall. Tramer led the way to us, high-stepping over the fallen mutants asleep on the floor. Several men followed him, too.

"They're with us," Tramer said as he came closer.

"They're…Xol?" Luke asked, his head shaking side to side as he eyed Tramer and then the three men in masks.

"Yeah." Fox reached us, his serious gaze checking out Luke as he staggered in his position. Jonah and I dodged over to help him stand. "Need some help?"

"How are they Xol and not…" Rosa asked.

"Insane?" Tramer offered.

"How are they not part of their cult?" I asked, gesturing to Tami on the ground. All the Xol patients were conditioned to their will.

Fox whistled and another militant came closer. While the rest of the two dozen soldiers went through the hallway, stopping to cuff the Xols, Fox and his comrade took Luke from my and Jonah's shoulders. "Better patch you up before your girl sees you faint."

Luke deadpanned at the teasing jibe in the Special Forces pilot's tone.

"Two of them are military hostages who were given the treatment against their will. Seems Interpol had files on them. The third"—Tramer gestured to a black guy who was restraining a couple of disgruntled human lab techs still standing—"is a former prisoner who escaped the Xol facility he was at for tests, and then came to the FBI. Confidential case. They'd tried those blue darts on him and missed, so he kept it. Then he gave it to a former Daysun technician who helped make those blue gas bombs."

"Dale knew about this?" Luke demanded, his tone accusatory.

Tramer shook his head. "Nope. A…certain hacker located the independent lab who was creating them." He shrugged. "Our man Zero knows *a lot* of people—or how to get their attention."

Damn. And those two hostages—probably prisoners of war—who'd be forced into Xols and to serve… *So messed up.*

Dale had mentioned Xol recruits being used in the military. Top-secret, of course, and for nefarious gains and personal profits, I was sure. How much could Tami and Michael have *sold* Xol-powered men to serve in violent ways?

"How the hell…" I laughed, the breath of relief nearly bowling me over. Giddy euphoria claimed me, almost to a narcotic high. I felt weightless, lighter than I'd ever experienced as it really hit me.

Surrounded by men prepared for combat, and aided by Xol mutants who weren't evil…

This was the end.

This was *it.*

We were safe, at last.

No more running. No more guessing. No more fearing the worst and facing something even more wicked than that. No more Xol freaks or Xol masterminds on the loose.

"We've got a lot of catching up to do, huh?" Tramer said with a rare smile.

Luke squeezed my hand, and like every time his contact grabbed me in the possessive and protective way, my heart beat faster. I squeezed back and dared to smile. A true, honest-to-God grin.

"Stay with me?" he asked.

I snorted. "Like you'll get rid of me now."

"Let's get you fixed up," Fox said, glancing at all of us. "And you." He eyed the cut on my lip and I couldn't believe I'd forgotten that Tami had struck me.

"Her first." I let go of Luke's hand to step back to Rosa. She was still standing there, pressing her palm to her side. As I moved toward her, she inhaled a deep breath and reached for me.

The strength of her thin arms around me surprised me, and I allowed myself the chance to soak in her hug. She'd never been quick to show affection, especially not in displays as physical as this. Now I knew, though, that she'd loved me more than life itself, that she'd gone to extremes to keep me safe from things she probably still wished she could have spared me from even knowing about.

"Thank you," I said into her hair as I held her tight.

She shook her head. "For what?"

"For being my mother."

She sniffed, and I held her as she cried.

****

It didn't surprise me that Luke refused to cooperate with the medics.

My man wasn't a pushover by any stretch of imagination, and if I hadn't been there with him, holding his hand, I doubted he would have even let them tend to his wound.

I kept my fingers threaded with his, not because he wasn't brave enough to face his injuries being accessed and tended to, but more, I felt, because he refused to let me out of sight.

It was a mutual addiction. Staying with one another. After the raw way I'd been kidnapped, and what was likely a nerve-wracking ordeal of him getting to me, we needed the obsessive reassurance that we weren't going to disappear on each other any time soon.

Fox and another of his team had helped carry Luke out of the Xol labs. Rosa was taken to an ambulance, and it had been a tricky moment of deciding where I belonged. The two people who mattered most to me were in different directions.

"Go on," Luke said. He looked up from his seat on the gurney in the ambulance. He must have noticed me glancing back and forth between the two vehicles with their doors open. Rosa lay on the gurney, talking to the medic who checked her blood pressure.

"She needs you," he said, nodding at the other ambulance.

But…I need you.

He almost smiled, that aw-shucks charming grin. "I do, too, but you're coming back to me."

Overwhelmed with love and the comfort of knowing I belonged to him, I climbed into the back of the van. I gripped his face, relishing the warmth of his cheeks between my hands, and brought my lips to his.

He groaned at the hard kiss and clutched my shirt. Before I could fall into his lap, someone cleared his throat behind me.

Jonah grinned, avoiding looking at us. "Maybe I can get a ride with someone else."

"No." Luke stared at me with a heady intensity that revved me too hot for what should be appropriate in an ambulance. Too needy for him when he was shot. He roved a slow stare over me, settling on my lips as he said, "I'll get my turn with her later."

Forever.

I smiled softly, grateful for his consideration of Rosa needing someone to comfort her too.

Jonah exchanged spots with me, going in to wait with Luke in his ambulance while I headed to Rosa's.

From the building, local police led cuffed patients into buses. Most were still wearing hospital gowns, but some had blankets protecting them from the night air. One by one, all these people who'd been transformed by the Xol treatment, most likely many with the Last Time dose, were now in the hands of the police. It was a hectic frenzy of officers and agents out here under the moonlit sky. Choppers flew above, probably the news. Acronyms on vests and coats flitted back and forth in the busyness. SWAT,

FBI, NARC, and various levels of federal and California law enforcement.

As corrupt as Project Xol was, I doubted all these first responders could be legit. I hoped though, that with Tramer involved, the leadership from at least one direction could be trusted.

As long as they're going far away from me. *Away from my loved ones.*

I sighed, picking my way through the foot traffic, and came to Rosa's ambulance. She rested there peacefully, watching me approach.

"So, Luke, huh?" she asked.

A blush stole up my cheeks and I shrugged. No. Screw that. No more shyness or silly reactions. I wasn't ashamed of Luke, or that I'd hooked up with him. Meeting him had changed my life for the better.

"Yeah. Luke."

She raised her brows and her mouth twitched, like she was biting back a smile. "He's…an unlikely match for you."

I smirked, waiting her out.

"He's so…rough, and he has such an…ugly past."

"And now he and I have one hell of a past together." Because it was in the past. Xol was over for me. It had to be. My mother—or any other scientist—could go to hell before they'd use me as their personal pawn for power.

"Go on," she said, waving at me to leave. She'd borrowed Luke's exact words and I couldn't help but laugh at the coincidence. I was determined to support them in the immediate aftermath of tonight's horrors but they didn't want to claim me. I wasn't so silly to think they didn't want me, only, they respected that the other might need comfort more.

Two giving souls. And they were both mine to keep in my life.

"Go on, go on." She smiled softly and then yawned. "We'll reconvene shortly. I'm sure we're heading to the same place now."

If she hadn't seemed so normal, walking, talking, and not expressing pain, I would have hesitated to leave her. None of us knew exactly what

Tami had used for the poison—what kind of lethal chemical she was slowly killing her with. With one final look back at her, checking that she seemed content and safe in the hands of the medic at her side, I left.

It was a crowded fit in the ambulance, with an EMT on Luke's left and me on the right. Jonah opted to ride with Fox, but Rosa had been right. We'd been taken to the hospital, a *legit* place for healthcare, and I'd waited while Luke's leg was examined.

Through and through again. Once the site wounds were cleaned, he was stitched a bit and given painkillers and antibiotics.

Reveling in the simple comfort of Luke's touch and a moment to simply breathe without anyone demanding anything of us, I sighed deeply.

Knocks sounded on the door before Jonah entered. "Dale's waiting for us at the hotel. He says it's nuts out there. As soon as you're clear to go, we'll fly over."

"Fly?" I asked.

"Chopper. Media's swarming the hotel lobby. It's *nuts* nuts."

"What's going on?" I asked Luke.

"Dale teamed up with your computer geek to expose Project Xol," Jonah said.

"Computer *geek*?" I sassed back. If he was referring to Zero, that was a gross understatement of what my friend was capable of.

"Zero's been helping Dale." Luke shifted to sit and swung his legs over the side of the bed.

"Easy," I warned him.

"I'm sick of waiting to get out of here."

I rolled my eyes. Yeah, he was the most impatient man on earth. But I needed to make sure he was okay to recover elsewhere.

"Reminds me of…" He rubbed at his face.

"The Xol place?" I asked, smoothing my hand over his back.

Jonah shook his head. "Prison?" he guessed.

Luke nodded. "After Ryan… When they'd patched me up."

I scooted closer to hug his side. It was still hard to accept Luke had endured nightmares of a different kind in the time *before* he'd met me and embarked on our crazy journey to end Project Xol. It wasn't fair for him to have suffered and lost so much this far in his life, but I vowed then and there that I'd be there with him to ride out every bad memory or any flash of anger.

Because he's already doing the same for me.

After I pressed a kiss to his shoulder, I said, "We'll go as soon as we can."

"Rosa's been discharged," Jonah said. "Told me to tell you she'll meet you guys there. Dale's anxious to speak with her."

Curiosity sparked, the idea of Rosa reuniting with Dale after so many years apart. Dale had kept in touch with Hendrick, and it was through their friendship Rosa was still somewhat informed of Tami's progress with testing and unethical experimentation. But…would she be mad at the billionaire? Annoyed with him, perhaps, for feeding

Hendrick with the intel and indirectly resulting in his death?

Within another half-hour, Luke was discharged, seeming to supremely piss off the nurse who was trying to read through his home recovery details line by line. The woman must be new to the job, because he surely wouldn't be her only patient hellbent on getting out of there.

Once we arrived at a hotel outside the hub of LA, Jonah led us to a suite where we found Dale speaking with Rosa on the couch. Tramer lounged on a chair opposite of Fox. At the end of the half-circle of plush furniture another man rested. Hands behind his head, legs sprawled out and crossed at his ankles, he seemed completely at ease. Calm.

Funny. I wouldn't think *calm* suited Xol mutants with their skewered hormones and unreliable moods. It was the tall, tan-skinned Xol who'd arrived at Tami's lab, one of the men Tramer had introduced as a former hostage from overseas. Seeing him without the mask was deceiving because he almost looked…human.

He is human. I held back a frown at my judgment. *He was a human. And now he's...something more.* Whether he could be trusted remained to be seen, but if these people gathered in this room could take faith in his loyalty, I'd try to as well.

"There she is." Rosa gestured to me and started to stand.

"No, no. Sit," Luke said. He headed toward them, using his crutches with ease, and claimed a seat next to Dale. I perched on the armrest of the couch, not caring if it made me seem clingy to Luke.

I crossed my arms and sighed. "So who's going to tell me what's been going on?"

Dale laughed once and shook his head.

"Girlie, you have scared about thirty years off my damn life."

I grinned at Zero's voice. Facing the phone lying screen-up on the coffee table, I replied, "Z, you have no idea how much I miss you." How long had it been since I'd hung out in his apartment, or brought him his favorite macchiato from Starbucks, or caught snippets of jazz down the hall?

Too long.

"Miss? I've been with you throughout this whole fiasco."

And without him, I had no clue where I'd be.

"Thanks, Z, for—"

He tutted. "Not yet. Not yet. We've only just started."

Between Zero and Dale, I learned that those two were taking *whistleblower* to an entirely new epic level. That would explain the news choppers hovering over Tami's facility that fast, and the mob of press flooding the hotel lobby.

Dale had been on the phone nonstop, pulling in favors and even bribing his associates. From a couple of congressmen, to foreign ambassadors, to various pharmaceutical corporations, he'd been in touch with numerous people who helped to spread the word of the top-secret agenda Tami had worked on since she'd faked her death. The science and medical fields were lit with the scandalous news.

Zero had the task of sharing proof of Project Xol's corruption. It was a trail as long as it was layered. Dismantling Project Xol wouldn't happen in one night, but I had no doubt Zero would ferret out every single crime and wrongdoing they'd committed in their attempt of creating a new subspecies of regenerative humans.

I'd shared my side of the story as well, explaining what happened since I woke up in the plane. Rosa collaborated details with me, and when I'd discussed Tami's specific speech about wanting to use my eggs, Rosa lashed out in Spanish profanity.

Tramer filled us in on his part in the rescue as well. He'd killed the Xol who'd taken the vial—which was smashed in the jungles of Mexico. How he'd ended the freak's life… Well, some things were too gory to willingly listen to. Hearing that the remaining vial was gone was the last nail of victory. No more readily accessible sources of that coveted beta DNA. The axolotls remained in their native habitat, and I supposed as long as they lived, the threat would remain to those who knew of their research possibilities.

As soon as Tramer saw to the destruction of that vial, he'd called Fox for transport, and by that time, they'd learned of a request for a delicate hostage rescue—me, in Tami's lab. It was a perfect overlap that Dale had spoken with his acquaintances, the right ones, it seemed, because Fox was tasked with rounding up a team of elite retired soldiers ready to fight at a moment's notice.

Our "meeting" lasted well past the night and into the morning. Only once we were all up-to-date with everyone's role of the night, we agreed to part ways. In a matter of hours, Dale was scheduled for a press conference, with Rosa at his side. As a remaining member of the original Xol research team, she was a source of many answers and her predictions would be trusted. Tramer and Fox needed to debrief with superiors, and many of the people behind the scenes of blowing up Project Xol would be meeting with all of us respectively. For the short term, Jonah, Luke, and I were spared having to give our statements to the stratified demands from various government branches. After we settled some, we'd be expected to share our stories to further the widespread investigation into Project Xol.

"I have to head back," Jonah said. "I mean, not today." He yawned, standing from his seat. I'd slumped down to wedge next to Luke, comfily trapped between his hard, hot body and the plush softness of the couch armrest. "My front desk guy said reporters are already showing up at the gym."

Our names had been slipped in the news of our involvement in the mass arrest at the Xol lab. In result, the brothers' last name garnered some unexpected PR for Jonah's gym. Ripples of after-effects of the Project Xol frenzy would likely last for a while.

The rest of the people in the room bade their goodbyes, needing sleep. Rosa was given the room next to the suite. Tramer and Fox, along with the "good" Xol, went to the floor below us for hastily-prepared vacant rooms. At least the hotel was more than accommodating with us camping out here for the night—day. Whatever. I'd lost track of the time, but my body was insisting on sleep. Seated next to Luke had calmed me enough that I was sure I *could* sleep.

"You guys sticking around here for long?" Jonah asked.

I shrugged. I had no clue what was coming next, and as long as Luke was with me, I didn't care much what happened.

"Maybe for a day. I don't want to fly too soon with my leg like this," Luke admitted. He shifted and I cringed at his hiss of pain.

I patted his good thigh. "Come on." I pushed to stand. "Jonah? Do you think he can get up?" I held out Luke's crutches and looked at Jonah expectantly, waiting for him to crouch over and help his brother stand.

"Pretty sure you're better at answering that than me."

Luke groaned and pretended to kick out at him with his uninjured leg.

I shook my head, smiling at his lameness.

"And here I thought you weren't some young punk anymore," Luke said.

Jonah chuckled, helping Luke stand. "Come on. She walked right into that one."

Luke rolled his eyes, accepting his crutches. "Good night," he said as he followed me out the main room of the suite. Halfway across the baby-soft, high-ply carpet, I paused in the short walk to the room Dale had said we could have. I turned around and returned to Jonah.

"Even if you *can* be too much sometimes," I said and reached on my tiptoes to press a kiss to his cheek, "thank you. For helping us."

One side of his lips tipped up in a smile and he patted my back. "You take care of him, all right?"

I nodded and went back to Luke.

"Remember you're on light duty restrictions, man."

Luke shook his head again at his brother's words. I grinned, enjoying this banter between the siblings.

We were silent in the room. Unlike the last time we'd had a chance to be alone with each other, this setting was nice. I didn't care if the room was fancier and elegant compared to the place in Xochimilco. It had a bed, I had my man, and we needed to sleep.

We didn't waste energy on words. Maybe because we were spent on sharing our stories of what had happened in the time we'd been apart, or because we were beat—physically and mentally. As we moved in sync, anticipating what the other needed, I realized we were just that tuned in to each other. Grounded in each other's presence and tender touch, we took our time undressing and stepping into the spacious stall with double showerheads. In any other circumstances, I would have taken the moment to appreciate and *ooh* and *ahh* at such a posh spa-like room.

With Luke's injury, and our fatigue, we simply cleaned up. Every touch of his taut skin and rock-hard muscles was like a gentle reacquaintance of him, promising me in the bare flesh that he was here. With me.

Forever.

I swallowed hard as he hugged me tight to him, his slick skin sealing our bodies together. He sighed, and I feared he'd topple over asleep right then and there, if not for the erection prodding at me to prove he was very much alert in one obvious way.

"I love you," he said on another long exhale. "I love you, Cassidy."

My heart thudded faster. For the first time in too long, I was revved up not by fear or adrenaline, but at the thrill he matched my feelings.

I had no reason to worry that he wouldn't be able or willing to have something more than a month of being on the run.

Love.

He was in this as deep as I was.

I craned my neck, bringing my face to his. Our long kiss was slow and tender, a perfect preview of what I wanted with him. Him, and every facet of him that was both gentle and rough.

"I love you, too," I whispered against his lips.

He rocked his hips against me. “So now what? You’ll have to teach me how this works.”

“Oh?” I kissed his neck and he growled, gripping my ass. The man needed *no* help in that department.

“I’ve never had a girlfriend before.”

I hummed, spreading more kisses down to his shoulder. I’d be more than happy to be his first. And only.

“Now what?” I answered his question with an echo.

For once, we were free to do whatever we’d want. No more letters pleading for my help. No more requests for retrieving things long-since buried. Nothing but each other.

“Besides abiding by your light-duty restrictions?” I ground against him, hitching my breath at the friction between us.

“Nothing is ever going to hold me back from you.”

I couldn't reply until he was satisfied he'd stolen my breath with a kiss even headier and more urgent than the previous one.

"Now…" I leaned back and gazed into his intense stare. The depth of love I felt in his embrace, under his scrutiny…it consumed me. I could only answer honestly. "Now we love each other."

He grinned a mischievous smile, the hard angles of his face softened under the water streaming down. With a slow nod, he leaned down to whisper, "Forever."

EPILOGUE

CASSIDY

One year later…

"Luke." I gasped his name as he hitched my skirt up. My back slammed against the edge of a bookcase and I winced before grinning. Pleasure and pain…he always made sure it was the former he gave me in the end.

"Uh-huh," he whispered at my neck. He sucked hard at my skin and I closed my eyes, gripping his hair. "I'm right here."

"That's the problem."

I felt his smile against my collarbone. He hoisted me higher against the bookcase in the back corner of the bookstore. The move caged me to him and freed his hand.

My panties weren't any defense against his fingers as he teased my already wet entrance.

"Problem?" he taunted. With his teeth, he yanked my shirt open more. "It doesn't feel like there's any *problem* here."

I gritted my teeth, falling into need for him despite my better logic.

"You can't just storm in here and…and…"

He covered my nipple with his mouth, laving the peak through my bra.

"Oh, my God…" I clutched his head to me, arching into his wicked intentions.

"I sure as hell can come in here and love on my wife. Whenever I damn well want to."

I whimpered as he thrust his fingers into me, circling his thumb at my clit.

This wasn't the fast, frantic rush through foreplay we normally found time for. He was dragging out his caress, slowly stoking and blowing more fuel into the fire of desire.

Which, damn, I missed the luxury of making love with my husband like there was no tomorrow. But—

"I'm at work." I panted as he shifted. His zipper seemed deafeningly loud in the small indie bookstore I'd started working at after I'd moved to Cincy with Luke months ago.

"And seeing as you're the manager, I've got all the permission I need here."

Unlike the way he needed the say-so for sexy time at home.

"Anyone could come see—"

He silenced me with a kiss as he drove deep into me. I keened into his mouth, wishing I could be quiet. Just once, to keep the volume down. His tongue dueled with mine as he slammed into me again. Faster and faster.

We broke for air and our ragged breaths only turned me on more.

No matter how fast or slow we could take it, my man never failed to drive me crazy. I'd never admit it to him, but yeah, going at it hard and fast in this hidden nook was filthy and unexpected, and I loved it.

We came together in a flash of drugging perfection. Sated, I relaxed in his arms. He pushed me against the bookcase some more as he caught his breath, his hot exhales whipping at the cooling wetness he'd left on my bra. As he came down from his orgasm, he leaned into me even more, as though he couldn't stand. My legs were shaky too, wrapped around his hips, but I hugged him to me, letting him recover. He heaved out a deep breath and the motion shifted my back toward the books behind me. One hardback fell down and he jerked his face up at the loud noise.

I stared at him, widening my eyes. I clamped my lips into the sternest mock-scowl I could manage. His eyes burned with laughter and he chuckled once. "Don't blame me."

"Oh. Right. Because I wasn't back here minding my own business, doing my job…"

He released me, kissing me gently until I was on my own two feet again.

"No, you can't." He tucked himself back into his pants and helped me adjust my clothes. "Blame those angels sleeping in your office."

I knocked my head side to side, granting him that point.

Elle and Hendrick *were* sweet angels when they slept. If only the twins could sleep *at night*. Or at any other predictable hour of the day.

No one said having babies would be a breeze.

"Mrs. Phelan is watching them today?" he asked.

I'd only just returned to work. The three months I'd given myself as maternity leave held many precious moments I'd treasure forever. But I'd been ready to ease into working a day or two for sanity. Mrs. Phelan had closed her bookstore in Ann Arbor and moved here to be *my* assistant. So besotted with the twins, she offered to watch them in the nursery area I'd set up in the office. It was the perfect arrangement, because as much as I wanted some me-time to work, I'd hated the idea of not being by my babies. Jonah and Luke made quick work of renovating the office for my needs.

Luke couldn't blame our twins for all the obstacles to our sex life—which was damned fine, if you asked me. The brothers had been busy over the last year. Dixon Gym's business exploded, and Jonah just opened a new branch in another town. Their reno work of flipping houses was still their side gig, and it was a miracle Luke and I had been able to compromise our lives as a couple.

We had a small marriage ceremony a month after we'd destroyed Tami's goal of starting a new generation of regenerative Xol mutants. Rosa, Tramer, Dale, and Jonah were the only guests, with Zero officiating. One month after that, we'd learned that we had babies on the way.

Elena Dixon was the easy one, but delivering our little boy was a pain like no other.

So if we're going to keep this up…we need to think about spacing out kids.

Elena Casal hadn't lived to meet our gorgeous little girl.

In the series of information we gained after that fateful night outside LA, we learned that she'd died. Even though Tami had given her Last Time, to prevent her from death, the initial stab wound to her heart was too hard to repair. Every time the regeneration process tried to override the injury, scar tissue prevented a full regeneration. When we'd heard of her demise, I'd been thankful she wasn't stuck in an agonizing limbo of a body both failing and regenerating over and over.

"Is Rosa still coming in to visit tonight?" he asked me as we walked to the office.

"Yeah. Dale too."

While my mother wasn't showing any sign of romantic intimacy with the CEO who had since restarted Project Xol, she was certainly rebuilding a friendship with the man.

In the year since Project Xol had been exposed to the world, Rosa and Dale relaunched the science—carefully and cautiously. The pipedream of a cure for cancer was too big to ever ignore, but this time, there were multiple levels of ethical checks and balances to prevent anyone like Tami to ruin the hope again. Last we'd heard, they were almost done inventorying the DNA of all the axolotl subspecies in the Xochimilco Lakes. There was sure to be a years' wait for a testable cure again, but it was a step in the right direction.

I slept at night knowing Tami, Michael, Jolene, and others behind the Project were behind bars. It took unique and extreme measures to truly keep them locked up, but I had to have faith they were never leaving their specially made prisons. Many charges were pressed against the people behind Project Xol. All over the world, men and women were brought to light as perpetrators of the unethical torture and handling of Xol patients. It seemed that each time someone was busted, it shed light on another scandal—a true network of corruption and evil that would require diligence and time to erase from the earth.

Luke opened the door to the office. Mrs. Phelan rocked Hendrick against her chest. She raised a finger to her lips, shushing as she sat in the rocking chair, keeping our boy asleep. Against the pale green walls with stencils of monkeys and trees, the babies slept.

"Want a break?" Luke asked her quietly.

She sighed and nodded. "I do need to use the restroom." She giggled and gave him a beseeching wince.

He smiled and gently scooped our son into his arms.

Mrs. Phelan patted my shoulder as she hurried past me out of the room.

I leaned over the portable crib Elena—Jonah nicknamed her Elle and it stuck—slept, one thumb in her little mouth.

Dammit. I winced, wishing I could nip that bud earlier than later. She flat-out wasn't taking to pacifiers and I had already settled myself in for giving up that fight.

I caressed her soft cheek and sighed.

Every time I looked at these infants, I lost a little of the fear that had once consumed me. That Tami could have succeeded, taking the idea of them from me before they were even conceived. With the unusual threat Tami had posed to me—to my body—I felt an extra sense of redemption knowing that Luke and I had created these beings.

Such a young, precious life, just starting out to what I hoped would be great things in her lifetime. Only *one* lifetime, an existence that wouldn't be extended by so-called drugs and cures that were actually a means for a psychopath's quest for dominance.

A fountain of youth. Project Xol had exposed one with grave side effects.

Gazing at my husband with our son in his arms, and then at our daughter sleeping with what I hoped were sweet dreams, I knew how pointless that search had been.

I met Luke's gaze and knew more than ever that anyone seeking immortality or power over others had never been so blessed as I was.

Because living with my husband's love and the gift of our children, I saw that it was only how we treasured each present moment that mattered.

AMABEL DANIELS

AMABEL DANIELS

AMABEL DANIELS

AMABEL DANIELS

AMABEL DANIELS

AMABEL DANIELS

ACKNOWLEDGMENTS

For editing, I thank C.J. Pinard at www.cjpinard.com. For the cover design and photography, I thank Kellie Dennis at Book Cover By Design at www.bookcoverbydesign.co.uk. For proofreading, I thank PSW.

For all the never-ending encouragement, suggestions, and cheerleading, I thank my great team of betas: Allyson, Crystal, Kirsten, Dawn, Julie, and Anna. I treasure your input and am so glad to have you in my corner!

ABOUT THE AUTHOR

Amabel Daniels lives in Northwest Ohio with her patient husband, three adventurous girls, and a collection of too many cats and dogs. Although she holds a Master's degree in Ecology, her true love is finding a good book. When she isn't spending time outdoors, or wondering how to negotiate with her mightily independent daughters, she's busy brewing up her next novel, usually as she lets her mind run off with the addictive words of "what if…"

For more information about Amabel's work, please stop by www.amabeldaniels.com.

OTHER BOOKS BY THE AUTHOR

Project Xol
Seek
Lost
Find
Stolen
Reclaim
Given

Newland Series
Better Than the Best
Appetite of Envy
Resisting Redemption
Covert Identities
Don't Go Back

Indeed

Always Was

Flawed Plan

Across From You
Next To Me

Olde Earth Academy
Secrecy
Discovery
Mastery
Victory